Stars in Chains
Book One: Slave

By
Herbert Grosshans

Published by
Melange Books, LLC
White Bear Lake, MN 55110
www.melange-books.com

Stars In Chains, Book 1, Herbert Grosshans Copyright © 2010, 2011
ISBN 978-1-61235-021-9

Credits

Editor: Tom Dahedl
Copy Editor: Nancy Schumacher
Format Editor: Mae Powers
Cover Artist: A. Brat

Stars in Chains
Book One: Slave
By Herbert Grosshans

Abducted, Earthman David Stark is sent to the mines on an alien planet. After escaping and a brief time of happiness in the arms of T'Phira, the Golden Goddess and in the City under the Ocean, he is captured again and sent to a planet of hot deserts populated by ferocious predators.

Visit Herbert's website:

http://hegro.shawwebspace.ca
http://hegro.blogspot.com/

Works also by and including Herbert Grosshans:
Stardogs 1 & 2
The Xandra Triology
Cliffs of Time
Orion the Hunt
Beyond the Stars Digest
Orion: Symbiont of Passion
Men of Eros

Stars in Chains
Book One: Slave
By Herbert Grosshans

Chapter One

"David Stark…"

The voice sounded sweet, soft, and alluring.

"Come…" whispered the voice again. He tried in vain to see the caller through the dark, gray mist.

Then he saw the eyes.

"No!" he cried out. "Something is wrong. The eyes…they are wrong!"

"Come, David," called the soft voice.

The eyes! He knew what was wrong with them. They were the eyes of a cat; large and blue, they glowed with a soft fluorescent light, but the face was human and beautiful. And familiar.

"David…"

The mist thickened, taking away the image. Floating in a void, frozen in time and space, his sluggish, heavy limbs wouldn't obey commands to move them.

"David…"

Drifting in the black void, the voice seemed far away. A bright light appeared suddenly and he reached for it. His hands grasped at nothing at first, but then he felt substance, clung to it. He heard a loud sound, like an explosion. His eyes opened, stared into the darkness.

Realizing he was awake, he sat up and looked around the room. He was alone; from outside came the sound of traffic. The rumbling of a muffler faded away in the distance. The explosive sound that had awakened him must have been the sound of a car's motor backfiring. There were still people who insisted on driving old, gas-guzzling clunkers. He closed his eyes for a moment; the afterimage of the strange eyes still burned in his mind.

There it was again. The same dream that kept haunting him every night for the last couple of weeks. He'd had nightmares before, ever since the Union War in South America in 2020. Ten years is a long time to forget, and he had forced those memories out of his mind, but his dreams kept coming back.

He looked at the clock on the night table.

The screen showed 1:00 AM.

He tried to get back to sleep but sleep wouldn't come. Restlessly he turned and turned until he finally got up. Something seemed to urge him outside. "I need to go for a drive," he murmured; quickly dressing he went into the garage to his car.

The Luxar purred softly as the engine sprang to life. Slowly, he eased the car out of the garage and pulled into the street.

Traffic was light and he leaned back into the soft leather seat and turned down the window.

The cool air felt refreshing on his face.

He remembered the dream and shuddered.

I wonder if I'm finally cracking up. I thought I was over it.

The months spent in the South American jungle troubled him. He had been part of a Special Unit to free an American diplomat who had been kidnapped by Union Terrorists. He and his team had run into an ambush. The diplomat and his fellow soldiers were killed.

The terrorists left him for dead. He would have died had it not been for a band of Indios who found him and carried him away, deep into the jungle. He didn't remember much about it. The loss of blood and the pain, the terrible pain in his stomach where the bullets had hit him, kept him unconscious most of the time.

They took him to some people. There was something strange about those people. He couldn't remember what, but they were kind and saved his life.

The trauma of being near death suppressed the memory of the event. The little he remembered was hazy, unclear. But the reoccurring dreams kept reminding him of the things he wanted to forget.

There had been a girl. He remembered a dirty, little boy…

* * * *

"Hey, señor, would you like nice señorita? My sister. She pretty and know how to make señor happy. No expensive."

He had been drunk, and he followed the boy through dark alleys to a rundown shack. The girl appeared young, thin. She lay naked on a torn blanket. Her small breasts were firm and nicely shaped. He stared at her spread legs, at the inviting pink slit between them. Her swollen mound was covered with thick, black hair. Perhaps she wasn't as young as she looked.

Uncombed, her hair hung loose around a narrow face and curled down and around slender brown shoulders.

She gave him an empty smile and beckoned as he stood looking down at her. He was horny and drunk. Dropping his pants, he followed her invitation and fell between her open thighs. She spread her legs wide and curled her fingers around his hard mast.

Groaning, he let her guide him into her warm sheath. She was extremely tight and she gave a little whimper when he pushed into her, but then she lifted up and churned her thin body underneath him with wild movements.

He knew the boy was watching, but he didn't care. He was too drunk to care about anything.

He didn't last long. Stiffening in her embrace, he called out harshly when he felt his climax approaching. She pushed him off before he exploded inside her and took hold of his spurting penis.

Breathing hard, he lay on top of her for a moment. Then he rose and pulled up his pants. The boy held out a small brown hand and he put some bills into it…

* * * *

No! He shook his head. That wasn't it.

There had been another girl. One whose memory he tried to suppress.

His thoughts came to an abrupt halt.

A shape on the side of the road.

A girl…waving her arms.

His tires screeched as he hit the brakes. Before he realized it, he had stopped and backed up toward the girl who came running. He opened the door for her and she slid into the bucket seat.

"Hi, what are you doing walking on the road at this time of night?" Looking outside, he noticed there were no houses. Without comprehending, he had left the city.

She smiled shyly, hooding her eyes with one hand. "I ran away," she said with a soft voice. She had a strange, heavy accent. A strangely familiar accent.

"So you ran away," he said. Looking at her, he noticed that she was practically nude. She wore a transparent cape that didn't hide anything. Her large breasts strained against the soft material, and even in the dim light of the dashboard, he could see them clearly.

She wore a small red cloth around her hips, like a loincloth, to cover parts of her lower body.

He kept his eyes on the road, but the sight of her shapely legs and nude white hips made his loins pound with desire. He cursed under his breath for getting himself into this situation. *Picking up a naked girl-hitchhiker was never a good idea.*

"Would you get my cigarettes from the glove compartment, please," he said, trying hard not to stare at her brown nipples poking through the sheer material.

She reached into the glove compartment and handed him the package.

"Take one for yourself," he said.

She shook her head. "No, thank you. I don't smoke." She brushed her long black hair out of her face and looked at him for the first time.

An icy breath seemed to touch his mind as he looked into her eyes.

They glowed softly in the dark. She had the eyes of a cat.

The strange people in the Brazilian jungle. He remembered their eyes. They had eyes like the ones that looked at him now. The same eyes that haunted him every night in his dreams.

She smiled gently. Her hand reached out and touched his arm. "Hello, David. I finally found you."

Her soft voice awoke something in his sub consciousness. He remembered a girl—a girl with strange eyes and an enchanting voice. She had looked after his needs, feeding him and washing him, as he recovered from his wounds. Sometimes she sat beside his bed and sang for him with that sweet, alluring voice. One night she came to him…

* * * *

…Her warm body slid beside him under the covers and her gentle hands touched him. Her small breasts flattened against his chest and he sensed the fire inside her. He wanted to tell her to go away, but she covered his face with kisses. When her lips closed over his, she pushed her tongue into his mouth, while her hand stroked his penis until he hurt with desire.

He put her onto her back and slid between her opening thighs. His hard organ probed her puffed up mound, found the slit of her vagina. When he tried to push into her, she whispered, "I'm a virgin. Please, be gentle."

"A virgin?" his breath rasped in his throat. "I shouldn't," he groaned, fighting the desire to ram his hard member forcefully into her. "You're too damn young."

"I'm older than I look," she whispered huskily. "I just happen to never have been with a man before."

Only twenty-one, with little experience of his own, he was gentle as he forced his aching penis into her tight sheath. Crying out when he took her virginity she embraced him, sobbing softly. He stopped moving and just held her.

"Did I hurt you?" he asked with a hoarse whisper.

"A little, but I'm fine now," she whispered back and began moving under him.

It was over much too soon and when he pulled out she cried a little. He stroked her soft black hair and wiped the tears from her beautiful face. Her strange, blue eyes looked at him and she smiled sadly.

"Where did you get those eyes?" he asked.

She didn't respond, just looked at him with her cat's eyes. Suddenly, she laughed. "I was born with them, like all of my people." She spoke English with a heavy accent. Stroking his chest, she said, "Do you want to try again?"

She didn't need to encourage him. He was young and horny and her sweet voice and lovely face had bewitched him. Her warm body felt inviting in his arms, and when her soft thighs opened, he slid between them.

He looked up when he heard the opening of the door and watched a number of people come into the room. Frozen between the girl's clutching thighs, he stared at the group of men looking at him with their strange eyes.

The men were old. Old and sad.

He slid off the girl and pulled the covers over his nude body.

She got out of bed and stood there, her eyes downcast. "I failed," she whispered.

One of the old men smiled and touched her arm. "Don't be sad," he said gently. "You did not fail. You are still immature, not yet fully developed. Your own talents have not reached their full potential."

His strange eyes fell on Stark. "He is the one. We are sure. The old *Seer* is sure. It is not the right time."

Stark didn't understand what those cryptic words meant, and didn't really care. He was angry with those old men for bursting into his room like this. He was angry with the girl and with himself.

"What kind of weird people are you?" Stark shouted. "You could have shown a little decency and knocked before you came into my room. I'm grateful to you for saving my life, but that doesn't give you the right to…and anyway, it was all her fault. She came onto me like…" He groped for the right words. When he saw their sad but somehow understanding faces, he shrugged. "I'm sorry. I'm as guilty as she is. I could have refused."

The old me stood there, smiled, turned and left the room.

The girl came back and touched his hand. "Don't be sorry," she said with her soft, gentle voice. "We did nothing wrong." Then she left.

Stark never saw her again. The next day some Indios came and took him to a village, where he boarded a boat back to civilization.

He forgot about the girl. Or almost forgot about her, because she visited him in his dreams…

* * * *

"Hi, Feleena," he said. "It's been a long time."

"Yes, it has." She nodded. "You remembered, even my name."

He chuckled. "I've tried to forget about you. I nearly succeeded, but my dreams kept reminding me of you." His eyes lingered on her large, firm breasts. "You've changed." He grinned. "You've grown up."

She knew what he meant and smiled. "I guess I have grown. In more ways than you can imagine." She gripped his hand. "I never forgot you either, David." Her grip on his hand tightened. "I came looking for you." Her eyes were large and suddenly she looked scared. "Now I'm not so sure if I did the right thing. Because of me, you may be in great danger. Oh, if things only would have worked out the way my people planned."

"What things did your people plan for me?"

"I can't tell you, because it doesn't matter now." A shiver ran through her body. "I'm chilly and I'm tired. Can we go somewhere warm where I can rest for a while?"

He looked at the traffic signs outside, trying to get his bearing. "There is a motel not far from here, if I remember correctly. We can go there." He took his eyes off the road for a moment and glanced at her. "You said you were looking for me. How did you know I would be coming this way?"

She smiled mysteriously. "I knew because I called out to you. And here you are."

Shaking his head, he drove on, toward the motel he knew should be coming up soon.

I called out to you. What did she mean by that? What made him take this route? He remembered getting out of bed, restless, remembered driving away from his home, but he didn't remember how he ended up on this back road.

When he saw the lights of the motel, he slowed down and drove into the parking lot. The sign said *Vacancy*. He had hoped it would, but this was not such a well-traveled road. The chances of finding the motel filled had been small. Checking his watch, he saw that it was nearly three o'clock. The proprietor would not be happy to receive guests, even though the sign on the office door said *Open 24 hours.*

He got out of the car and waited for Feleena to come out on the other side. Looking at her exposed body, he took off his jacket and draped it across her shoulders.

"Thank you," she said, shivering in the cold air.

He smiled. "I didn't give you my coat because you're cold." Then he opened the door to the office.

The old man in the chair behind the counter opened one eye and peered sleepily at the two intruders who dared to disturb his snooze.

"We'd like a room for the night," Stark said.

"You would, wouldn't you," the old man wheezed, getting out of his chair. The gaze of his rheumatic eyes took in Feleena's half-naked body. "You and the Misses, I suppose? Will you be staying the whole night?"

"Not the whole night." Stark smiled, pretending not to notice the sarcasm. "Only what's left of it."

"Makes no difference. It'll still be eighty bucks. Cash."

Stark shrugged and took his wallet from his back pocket. Taking out four twenties, he put them on the counter.

The old man shoved them into his pocket, shuffled to the back wall and took a key from a hook on the board. Handing it to Stark, he said, "Room seven, the last on the left."

"Aren't you going to write my name into your logbook?"

Staring at Stark, the old man pulled his dry lips into a toothless smile. "We are not that formal in this place, Mister. I've never seen you before." He winked. "If you know what I mean."

Stark took the key and walked with Feleena out of the door. It didn't really matter what the old man thought.

The room was shabby; not worth the eighty bucks he had paid for it. The covers on the bed looked wrinkled and not too clean. When he tried to lock the door, it wouldn't lock. Shrugging, he left it unlocked. There was not much danger out here in the country for anyone to break into the room.

Feleena took Stark's jacket and threw it onto the only chair. Then she removed her skimpy clothing and, naked, she stood by the bed and looked at him, her cat's eyes large.

He stared at her nude body. She looked so perfect with beautifully shaped breasts and round, solid buttocks. A small patch of black, curly hair between her legs covered her well-developed Venus mound, hiding the slit of her pussy.

A sudden desire to take her into his arms made his loins throb and his heart beat faster.

She lifted the covers on the bed and slipped under them. "I'm chilly," she said softly. "Come to bed and make me warm."

The image of her nude body floated in his mind. He remembered her undeveloped form, her small breasts, and the way she had moved beneath him when he took her innocence. Something had happened between them that night, something more than just the loss of her maidenhead to his awkward thrusts.

She had seduced him then, just as she was seducing him at this moment. Her motive had never been clear to him, not then and not now. Even though they had been intimate that night in the Brazilian jungle, it had been a one-time affair. They had not been lovers, and yet…there was a bond between them that could not be explained or put into words.

He felt drawn to her. The time they had spent apart seemed to have vanished in an instant. The ache in his heart and his longing for her was stronger than ever. "I thought you were tired," he said.

"I've rested in the car, but I'm still chilly. I need a warm body to warm me up."

He undressed with trembling fingers, his sudden desire overpowering and impossible to control.

She giggled when she saw his erection and raised the corner of the bedcovers in invitation.

He took her into his arms, covered her face with kisses, unable to hold back. Her legs opened wide and he slipped between her soft thighs. His hard penis found the opening between them and, with a loud groan, he entered her wet, creamy pussy.

A feeling of happiness and fulfillment rose up inside him the moment the tight walls of her sheath closed around his throbbing piece of flesh.

Moaning, she wrapped her long legs around his hips, resting her heels on his flexing buttocks. "You don't know how often I've dreamed about this moment," she gasped into his ear.

They didn't speak for a long time, only their bodies moved in perfect unison, sensing each other's needs and wants. Thrusting and pushing, yielding and giving, like two lovers who had done this countless times before, they performed an act that was as old as life itself; nothing unusual or special, but unique in the fact that this was only the second time their bodies touched in an intimate embrace.

They were not lovers, only a man and a woman who barely knew each other, fucking their brains out. And yet…Stark somehow knew that there was much more to their chance encounter than appeared at the surface.

He pushed deep into her with every powerful thrust and she writhed underneath him, moaning, and whimpering as she responded to his animal lust with fiery passion.

Waves of pleasure vibrated through every fiber of his body, like tiny electrical shocks, building up to a roaring thunderclap as he freed the pent-up energy in one explosive release.

His shouts of pleasure blended with her ecstatic cries as he shot his hot discharge into her pulsating pussy. Her lips felt hot on his skin as she pressed her mouth against his throat, her teeth grazing his pulsating vein. A feeling of power and elation rushed through his entire being when he felt the sting of tiny pinpricks at the peak of their passion. His mind reached for the stars, drawing energy from the fabric of the universe.

It was over too soon.

He laid in her arms, breathing hard and fast, his heart beating in his chest as he came down from the euphoria that had filled his mind and body.

"That was wonderful," she whispered. "Better than in my dreams and better than the first time."

He chuckled into the hollow of her breasts. "I was young and inexperienced then, but I've had some practice in the meantime. I don't recall you being this passionate."

She laughed and stroked his back with gentle fingers. "I've also had some practice."

He didn't remember falling asleep, but when he opened his eyes and looked around the room he noticed light streaming through filthy, ripped curtains covering a small window. Suffering a moment of disorientation, he lifted his head and saw his jacket lying on the seat of an old wooden chair with a broken leg. The rest of his clothing lay in an untidy heap on the floor.

Shivering, he realized he was naked. Then he became aware of the woman lying in the crook of his arm and stared down at her, smiling, as he remembered.

"Feleena," he whispered.

She stirred. Her eyelids fluttered open. A ray of sunshine sneaked through a hole in the curtains and fell across her face, highlighting her blue strange eyes. She smiled lazily and touched his cheek. "I'm not dreaming," she said, her voice happy and content. "You are really here."

"Wherever here is," he chuckled. "That was quite some action," he said. "I feel drained. You certainly sucked me dry last night."

She laughed, slid on top of him, and pressed her nude body against him; moving down to his penis and fondled it. "You didn't exactly struggle," she said. Then she kissed him.

He felt his penis responding to her touch and didn't object when she straddled him. Sitting up, she looked down at him with a mischievous smile. "Seems to me someone is looking for a warm place."

She began rubbing her pussy over his hard penis. Closing her eyes, she moved her pelvis slowly back and forth, grabbing his mast with her soft labia and quickly dousing his pubic hair with warm liquid.

When she lifted up, his stiff penis stood free for a moment, abandoned and alone but not for long. She descended and impaled herself with one smooth motion. Then she began moving up and down, taking him deep into her with every downward plunge.

He watched her breasts jiggling gently on her ribcage as she rode him, slowly at first but with ever-increasing speed until her lower body was almost a blur.

Digging his hands into her soft breasts, he closed his eyes and concentrated on the spot that joined them together, his mind aware of nothing else but her fast-moving clutching sheath.

"Now," she called out. "Please come now!"

His penis jumped inside her clutching pussy as he exploded, shooting his discharge into her.

She cried out, sat quivering and whimpering in his lap, accepting him as he filled her vessel, her vagina walls constricting tightly around his throbbing penis. Sensing her forward movement, he opened his eyes to look at her descending face. Her mouth was slightly open, displaying long needle thin fangs. She nuzzled his neck, her mouth searching. He felt a slight pain, like a dentist's needle, a momentary stabbing sensation through his mind, then nothing but tremendous joy.

His penis was still rigid in the trembling folds of her hot pussy and incredible pleasure radiated from his pubic region in massive waves, filling his entire being with a feeling of euphoria as his mind expanded to become one with the universe.

Time stood still, nothing existed but joy and happiness. And a feeling of supreme power.

The noise of someone pounding against the door brought him back to reality. It took him a moment to focus on the sound and make him realize where he was.

The hinges of the door creaked as someone opened it.

Feleena crouched above him. Her mouth was open, red liquid colored her lips. Licking them, she hissed and turned her head to look at the intruder who stuck his head into the room. "What do you want?" Her voice sounded husky, demanding.

"Another eighty bucks, unless you vacate this room within the next five minutes."

Stark recognized the voice of the proprietor. He looked past Feleena to see the old man's rheumatic gaze gawking at her nude body.

"Second thought, if you let me watch for a while I might let you stay the rest of the day," the old man chortled.

"If you don't close the door within the next five seconds you'll be beyond caring if we stay or not," Stark said harshly. "I'm not paying you one more dime, you lecherous old man. This room isn't worth half the money I gave you."

"All right, all right. I'll let you finish up. Make sure you'll leave the room the way you found it, you lucky bastard." His chuckle sounded gleeful. "Just getting a good look at that lovely naked ass of the broad is payment enough for me."

After another leering look at Feleena, he closed the door.

Feleena laughed and rolled onto her back. Stretching her lithe body, she yawned and looked at Stark. "Too bad he interrupted us when he did. I have never felt this elated and happy." She smiled and ran her finger down his chest. "Did I make you happy?"

He sat up and studied her lovely face. Her eyes glittered with blue fire and full lips revealed white even teeth, not the fangs of a vampire capable of sinking them into a victim's throat.

"Did you drink my blood?" Feeling foolish the moment the words came across his lips.

Her mouth formed a sweet smile. "What makes you say that?"

He laughed, slightly embarrassed.

"Forget it. Just my overactive imagination. Comes from reading too many horror stories." He got up and sat at the edge of the bed. Looking around the room, he said, "What a dump! Not even a place to wash up. I hope they have at least a community washroom."

* * * *

"I must have been in a real trance last night. I can't remember leaving the city and driving down this forsaken road," he said, glancing at Feleena.

"How did you end up in this back country?"

She hesitated before answering.

"It is complicated and not easy to explain without revealing things you may not believe or even understand."

He didn't get a chance to answer her. His foot hit the brake petal when from a dark side road a car shot into his lane and blocked his way. "Damn it!" he cursed and swerved onto the shoulder to avoid hitting the other car. With screeching tires he barely managed to stop his car before landing in the ditch.

"What kind of a fucking idiot..." he yelled. Ripping open his car door, he stepped onto the gravel. He stopped briefly when he heard Feleena calling,

"David! Don't go. Run away!" However, he was too angry and ignored the urgency in her voice.

"I'm going to teach that son-of-a-bitch a lesson!" he snarled.

The doors of the other vehicle opened and two men jumped out.

Two big men.

"What the hell is the matter with you guys?" Stark slowed his advance, watching them with sudden apprehension. "Are you drunk or on drugs?"

The two men didn't answer. Like two silent shadows, they came closer. Stark had enough time to register their sickly white and expressionless faces before he let out a surprised shout when one of them hit him in the stomach with a fist as hard as a sledgehammer.

He doubled over and clutched his belly. "What the fuck!" he moaned, backing away.

His attacker looked at him with cold, glittering eyes and pulled back his fist again. Stark was prepared and moved to one side. He brought up his own fist, but before he could smash it into his opponents face, his companion had moved behind Stark.

He felt the impact when the man hit him hard behind the ears. He thought he heard a woman screaming as he lost consciousness, but he couldn't be sure.

Chapter Two

Dark shadows moved slowly around him. He tried to see but couldn't penetrate the fog.

Then he heard the voice.

"David…"

As he stared into the dark, he suddenly saw the outlines of a face. Two blue eyes gazed at him.

The face looked familiar. There was something about the eyes. They were not human. No human eyes have slit pupils.

Groaning, he forced himself to wake up, opened his eyes. That dream again.

His mind seemed to be in a haze. He had to concentrate to think clearly. He remembered being hit with a hard instrument. When he touched the spot behind his ear, he was surprised that he didn't find a lump or feel any pain. He stared at the blank ceiling above him, trying to remember what exactly had taken place.

Lifting his head, he discovered that he was lying on a polished floor, inside a small room. He didn't see a door in the smooth walls.

"Wonder where the hell I am," he mused and rose shakily to his feet. He took a couple of steps and nearly fell when he was yanked back by something that dug into his ankle. He looked down at the shiny metal band circling his leg and cursed again.

A chain connected to the metal band. The other end of the chain was attached to a ring in the floor.

"This is preposterous," he shouted, looking around the room. Even though he didn't see a door, there had to be one. Somebody put him into this room. He searched the ceiling and corners for cameras but didn't see any. There weren't any light fixtures and yet it wasn't dark. The ceiling glowed with an intense light, illuminating the room with cold brightness.

He felt a soft vibration running through the floor and became aware of a barely audible humming.

He grabbed the chain and yanked on it until his hands bled. "Someone is going to pay for this!" he growled, anger welling up inside him.

"Can anybody hear me?" he shouted. "Show your faces, you cowards!"

He stood in the center of the room, his fists balled at his side, listening, but everything stayed silent, the rattling breath coming from his throat the only sound.

Slowly, he calmed himself. Anger would not get him out of this situation. He needed to stay calm.

Everything seemed so surreal. Maybe he was dreaming. He dismissed that notion when he looked at his bleeding hands. This was not a dream. This was real, but where was he? Why was he chained to the floor?

Who were those two men who attacked him and why did they kidnap him? If this was a kidnapping then it didn't make sense. They had nothing to gain from keeping him hostage. He had no family who would pay for his release.

He thought about Feleena, recalling her last words.

David! Don't go. Run away!

Was she involved in this? Maybe they had been after her and he was only an innocent bystander at the wrong place at the wrong time.

A loud roar behind him made him swing around. Taking an involuntary step back, he stared at the creature only a few steps in front of him.

Nearly three meters tall, the beast appeared human at first, until he saw the head. Two eyes glowed with red fire inside deep sockets above a snout filled with long, dagger-like teeth. The giant creature, also shackled, glared fiercely and let out another terrifying roar. Yanking on its chain, the creature reached for Stark, but the chain kept the monstrosity at bay.

I hope the chain holds, he thought, as he looked around the huge room. The walls had disappeared and he saw that he was not alone. There were others in the room.

He jumped a little when someone touched him on the shoulder and turned around, lifting his fists to defend himself.

"Feleena?" he asked when he saw the girl. She still wore the transparent cape, but she was not nude underneath. Tight fitting pants and a loose blouse covered her body. A skullcap hid her long hair.

"Yes, David. It's me." She gave him a sad smile. "I'm sorry you got involved in this. It is my fault."

"How is it your fault? Are you mixed up with the people who abducted me?"

She shook her head. "Not in the way you are implying." Her hand touched his cheek. "I'm sorry."

"Who are these people? What do they want from me?"

"From you? Nothing. They wanted me."

"Why?"

"I can't explain it now. You'll find out soon enough." Her strange eyes searched his face. "Are you hungry?"

"I haven't given it any thought. Come to think of it my stomach does feel empty. We should have had something to eat at that dump after all this morning." He rubbed his chin and was surprised to discover thick stubble. "What time of day is it?"

"Probably morning."

"You mean I was out almost a whole day and night?" he asked, puzzled.

"More than that. Five of your days."

"I don't understand."

She gave him a cheerless smile. "I must go now. We'll be landing soon."

"What do you mean…?" He watched her as she rushed away, puzzled by her cryptic words.

We'll be landing soon?

This room couldn't be inside an airplane. *Could they possibly be on a ship*? Running his hand over the stubble on his chin, he wondered how he could have been unconscious for five days?

Sighing, he squatted on the floor, eyeing the giant creature on his left with trepidation. It was not a primitive beast as he had assumed at first. Animals don't wear clothes, not usually, unless their owners are among those who have the misguided believe that animals are people and enjoy wearing clothes. Clothes made from furs covered the creature's huge body. He noticed that the giant was watching him out of eyes showing more than animal awareness.

When he scanned the room, he saw other creatures. Many seemed human until he looked into their faces. There was nothing human about them. Some had trunks where the nose should have been, some had only slits above their mouths. One had large protruding eyeballs above a pig-like snout, and another one stared around with multifaceted eyes.

They all had one thing in common: all were chained to the floor.

A terrible thought was born inside him, and he did not want to think about it.

He was on board a spaceship that had been captured by aliens! It sounded crazy, but it was the only explanation he could find.

His thoughts were interrupted when the beast-man beside him let out a bloodcurdling roar and rattled his chain. When he looked for the reason of the creature's angry outburst, he saw a group of tall figures walking toward him. Underneath their capes they wore skintight black outfits.

They looked like men, but when he looked into their faces he knew they were not human. Black eyes glittered cold in skulls covered with smooth white skin. They didn't talk among themselves as they came closer. The group stopped and one of them walked toward the beast-man.

The monster growled deep in his throat and, with flashing teeth sprang at the intruder who dared to invade his space.

The beast-man never reached his intended victim. With superhuman speed, the stranger's hand dipped under his cape and retrieved what was clearly a weapon. A white, blinding light discharged from its spiral tip hitting the beast-man in the chest; crashing the creature to the floor without a sound.

Without giving the fallen creature a second look, the black-clad stranger stepped over the lifeless body and approached Stark. He bent and touched the metal band around Stark's leg. It fell open with a barely audible click.

He was free.

Stark looked at his rescuer, who glared at him with his cold eyes. When he didn't make a move, the stranger kicked him in the side with one iron hard fist and indicated for him to follow the other freed prisoners who were forming a line and moving toward an exit that had appeared in the far wall.

Reluctantly, he followed the order and joined the line. Guards carrying short sticks kept anyone who might be trying to escape from doing so by prodding the prisoners with their sticks. One of them touched Stark in the neck, and he suppressed a surprised shout as a painful electric shock nearly threatened to paralyze him.

When he stepped through the exit, he squinted against the glare of a bright blazing ball in the greenish sky. It confirmed his suspicion that he was on an alien planet. In the distance, he saw buildings rising into the sky. They were of unfamiliar designs, defying gravity and logic. Giant disks rested high above the ground on thin spiral columns, connected by flimsy appearing bridges. The air was buzzing with airborne vehicles that should not have been able to fly.

They walked on a shiny surface toward a row of tear-shaped vehicles. A guard pushed Stark into the first vehicle and, stumbling through the entrance, he kept from falling by clawing at the prisoner in front of him. The man-like being growled and showed him a row of sharp teeth, pushing Stark into another prisoner who clung to Stark for support.

By the time everyone was on board they were huddled together in a tight group, unable to move much. Stark took shallow breaths through his mouth to keep from gagging because of the unfamiliar and unpleasant odors oozing from his fellow prisoners.

A slight vibration ran through the vehicle. He couldn't see the outside. The walls were smooth and without windows, but he knew they were airborne. The flight didn't take long before he felt the vehicle descend again.

The oval door opened and the prisoners were told by one of the skull-faced guards to exit. Stark jumped onto the glass-like surface outside and walked with the other prisoners as they were herded toward one of the tall buildings he had seen from the spaceport.

Before they reached their destination, their guards ordered the group to stop. They began pulling a number of the prisoners out of the group, Stark among them.

As he stood wondering what was going to happen to him, a woman's voice called his name. He turned to see Feleena standing beside one of the guards.

"Come, David. Come with me."

"Where are we going?" he asked, throwing an anxious look at her escort.

She smiled sadly. "To meet the Almighty Kaloor."

"Is he the one responsible for my abduction?"

"In a way he is. Don't ask too many questions, not now." Her fingers dug into his arm. She threw him an anxious glance. "Keep your thoughts to yourself, please. Now, come."

"What is going to happen to them?" He indicated the other prisoners.

"Most of them will end up in the mines. The rest will be slaves to some rich nobleman. Those are the lucky ones."

"And I?" he asked. "What will happen to me?"

She sighed. "Yours and my destiny is not much better than theirs."

The guard with Feleena spoke a few words in a harsh language. His black eyes glittered in his expressionless white face. Then he turned and walked away.

"We need to go," Feleena said, pulling Stark with her.

Silently and deep in thought he walked at her side, wondering who this Almighty Kaloor was.

They followed the guard to a giant sphere floating a foot above the polished ground...obviously some kind of vehicle. The surface of the globe shimmered with fluorescent rainbow colors in the bright light of the alien sun. They boarded it through an oval door that opened as they approached.

From the outside, Stark had not been able to see the interior of the vehicle through the opaque walls, but once inside, the walls seemed to have disappeared. The sky and ground were clearly visible.

As soon as they took their seats, the sphere lifted and Stark suffered a short bout of vertigo as the ground underneath them sped away. He looked into the sky to regain his equilibrium but paid for that with the fear that they might collide with one of the many vehicles traveling with nearly impossible speed along invisible flyways.

They left the city behind and flew over vast forests and far-spreading savannahs. He saw other cities below them at almost regular intervals. After about a two-hour flight, Stark saw buildings rising into the sky in the distance. The buildings grew taller and more massive as the sphere neared them until they flew among the giant skyscrapers, seemingly dodging other airborne vehicles.

One of the buildings rising up in front of them changed into a massive solid wall of gleaming metal and plastic. When Stark thought they might hit the wall, a hole appeared and they entered the open space.

The sphere floated slowly between huge pillars and finally settled softly on the glass-like floor. There were other, similar vehicles already parked inside the huge area, and Stark couldn't help but compare it to indoor parking lots on Earth. In one way, it calmed him to know that things were not so unfamiliar on this alien planet.

Maybe everything would turn out better than expected. The creatures he had met so far didn't look human on the outside, but perhaps inside they were not much different from him.

The guard led them through a door into an elevator. It shot upward and stopped smoothly after a short trip to the top of the building.

The room they entered was furnished with things built out of wood, stone, metal, and plastics. Some of them massive and solid, decorated with sparkling precious stones, others flimsy and transparent, flowing toward the ceiling were they melded into a mass of shimmering and glowing drops. Those things could have been simply furniture or displays of art; expressions of inspiration conceived inside an artist with an imagination completely foreign to Stark's perception of beauty and way of thinking.

His eyes were drawn to the center of the room. When he looked at the being sitting inside a chair-like contraption, he drew in a deep breath, trying not to let out a sound of surprise.

The body, even though frail and emancipated, appeared human. So did the head, except for its size. It towered like a huge, white globe above the body, connected to it by a skinny neck. The skull was bald and transparent. Stark could see the brain pulsing inside the giant milky globe.

At first, he wondered how such a frail body could support the huge head, until he realized the being floated inside a tank filled with liquid.

The human-like face looked serene and with eyes closed, appeared to be sleeping.

"What the hell is that?" Stark wondered as he stared at the grotesque creature.

The eyelids fluttered open to reveal a pair of flaming eyes. They burned with green fire, and Stark had to squint as he looked into them.

"Kneel," Feleena whispered fiercely beside him. "And bow your head."

"I don't kneel in front of anyone," Stark said in defiance.

He cried out involuntarily when a heavy weight smashed into his neck. Staggering from the blow, he spun around, looking for his attacker but saw nobody behind him.

"On your knees, Worm!" thundered a voice.

A violent kick into the hollow of his knees forced him to sink to the ground. Suppressing a shout of anger and pain, he rested on his knees and hands, trying to regain his composure. He looked at the creature in the tank, his vision blurred from the painful blows.

"Kiss the holy ground you are standing on, Worm!" the voice thundered again.

Stark's head was forced to the ground until his face touched the floor. He resisted the invisible power but the effort was futile. Angry and helpless he felt his lips pressed against the cool surface of the hard polished stone.

The pressure was suddenly gone and he was free to move. Lifting his head, he stared into the creature's face. The thin lips under the flat nose formed a smile, exposing a ridge of white bone. The gesture did not convey good will; it was savage and arrogant.

The eyes had lost some of its fire but still blazed like a smoldering flame, ready to flare up.

"How dare you to feel pity for me? I could crush you like a crawling annoying insect with just one thought." The words seemed to hang in the air. He heard them but he hadn't seen the lips move.

"You speak my language?" Stark asked, not knowing what else to say.

Amused laughter rang through his awareness. "I don't. Language is not a barrier for me because I do not communicate by your primitive ways."

"How...?"

"I speak to you with my thoughts. I am inside your head." Again, that amused laughter.

"Does that mean you can read my thoughts?"

"Your thoughts are as open to me as if you had spoken them aloud. You cannot keep any secrets from me. I am all knowing and all-powerful. I am a god. What you experienced is only a small demonstration of what I am capable of." The eyes looked at Feleena. "You have been defiant, Slave. You tried to escape."

Feleena hung her head. "I beg your forgiveness, my Lord. I was looking for my parents."

"Your parents are dead, Slave."

"So I've been told. I was clinging to some hope. It was wrong of me to leave the ship without permission. It won't happen again. Please, have mercy, my Lord." Her voice sounded meek and without emotion.

"Your behavior has always been exemplary. Your songs have pleased me in the past. That is why I shall be lenient, but I believe a short time in the *Krestoll* mines will be of great benefit." He stared at Stark. "You will go with her as her protector. The mines are a rough place. You make certain nothing happens to her. Now leave my presence!"

The eyes closed and Stark became aware that the tingly feeling he had been aware of all this time was suddenly gone.

Feleena tucked on his arm. "Let's go, David. We've been dismissed. Lingering will arouse his anger."

With one last glance at the being in the tank, Stark followed Feleena. Their guard who had been standing silently behind them, walked ahead of them toward the elevator. He waited until they stepped into it before he joined them.

"What's the story with that oversized brain?" Stark asked.

Feleena gave him a warning look. "Speak and think only with reverence of the Almighty Kaloor. He can read your thoughts even if you're not in his presence."

Stark chuckled. "Somehow I can't believe that. As big as his brain is, he can't be everywhere at the same time. There must be millions of beings living in this city. If he would be aware of everyone's thoughts, he'd go nuts. He is not a god."

"He may not be aware of you but his servants are. The Melkos can also read thoughts. They are everywhere." She threw a worried glance at their guard who stood in the corner watching them. His white face was expressionless, like the face of a dead man, but his eyes were alive with glittering sparks.

Stark turned to look at the guard with sudden apprehension.

"He probably doesn't care what you think," Feleena said. "As long as your thoughts don't involve resistance or trying to escape." She caressed his arm. "Everything will be fine, David. I've been a slave for many years. It is not so bad. I'm glad you are here with me."

He gave her a thoughtful look. "I am not sure if I can say the same. Your god Kaloor is sending us to work in the mines. That doesn't sound like a good deal to me. By the way, you never did tell me why you were looking for me. I believe you have a lot of explaining to do."

She smiled. "Yes, I do but not here."

Chapter Three

They were put into a transport ship that would take them to the fifth planet where they'd be spending the next few months working in one of the mines digging for *Krestoll*.

"What is Krestoll?" he asked Feleena.

"A semi-precious stone that is used to power the great ships that travel between the stars. The fifth planet is rich on Krestoll. It is not a friendly planet."

"I hope it is warm there." Stark chuckled, trying to regain his sense of humor. "I didn't dress for cold weather." He indicated the short sleeves of his shirt.

Feleena smiled. "You are overdressed. The planet is uncomfortably hot and wet, the land mostly jungle and wild, with raging rivers and huge lakes. But there are also great areas of dry and hot deserts with nothing but drifting sand. Wild and ferocious beasts are everywhere, meat eaters mostly. Do you want to hear more?"

"I think I get the picture." He looked grimly at the other slaves who would share his and Feleena's fate. There were twenty of them. All of them were humanoid in appearance but only eleven had human-like features. The others seemed to have been created by a madman with a strange sense of humor. Two had long snouts filled with sharp teeth, their faces were covered with short hair, and their eyes shone black and alert as they surveyed their prison.

The heads of two others were long and narrow, alligator-like, connected to their bodies by short, sinewy necks. They had claws for hands and huge feet covered by thick scales. The only reason Stark assumed they were intelligent was the fact that their bodies were covered by thick robes that fell past their bony knees.

The three creatures at the far end could have been primitive apes had it not been for their skintight suits and the protective lenses over their eyes.

And then there was one who had no face. His head was shaped like a long cucumber with a tuft on the top. He had two eyes in the front and two in the back of his head. No mouth and no nose. None that Stark could see. His arms ended in thin strands, like a scarecrow's straw hands protruding from torn sleeves.

Even though none of them spoke, Stark smelled their fear. Unlike him and Feleena, they probably had no idea what waited for them. He wondered where they all came from.

"How long until we get there?" he asked Feleena.

"Not long." She pointed at his watch. "Maybe two more hours your time."

"My time," he repeated. Slowly, it began to dawn on him that he was in a spaceship that traveled from one planet to another in a matter of hours. He also realized that he was not in the Solar system anymore but in some star system far away where things were different from conditions on Earth. The planet he'd be living on would have longer or shorter years, with different seasons, depending on how long it took for the planet to circle its primary sun. The length of the day would not be the same. His body would have to adjust. His mind would have to accept the new things he'd experience.

He knew he could never accept being a slave and he would try to escape the first opportunity he'd get. He was not shackled, but there was nothing he could do right now, trapped inside a spaceship traveling through airless space. He had to wait until he was back on solid land with breathable air and hopefully a place where he could hide.

He glanced at Feleena who sat beside him. She hadn't spoken for some time now. He noticed her closed eyes and discovered he was suddenly quite tired. Until now he'd been running on adrenalin and his body was finally demanding payment. Closing his eyes, he leaned back on the hard bench and made himself as comfortable as possible.

* * * *

Uncomfortably hot and wet, Feleena had told him. A gross understatement. Stark's lungs rejected the alien air by refusing to let him breathe. Doubling over, he fought for breath and coughed until his body adjusted. His skin felt clammy and uncomfortable from the wet shirt plastered against his skin.

He noticed that a few of his fellow prisoners reacted the same way he did, some even more violently as they fell to the ground, gasping for air.

Feleena, who seemed to show no ill effects, grabbed his arm. "Relax and calm down," she said soothingly. "It will pass. Just give it a moment."

Her words helped and after a while, he felt quite normal as his body accepted the hot, humid, and somewhat acrid smelling air.

A number of armed guards herded the group of prisoners toward a low building that looked out of place amidst the tall plants seemingly waiting for a chance to prance on the intruder and assimilate it.

They didn't enter the building. All he prisoners had to line up in a row. One of the guards ordered them through gestures to take off their clothes. Not all followed the order; some either didn't understand or pretended not to understand. Only after a couple of guards began stripping them forcefully, they complied.

Watching the group, Stark noted that not all of the prisoners were males. He saw a few with breasts; obviously females.

Feleena stood beside him, as naked as the others. She looked so perfect, so lovely.

She saw him studying her and smiled but didn't say anything.

The guards handed each of them a pair of drab gray coveralls. Stark slipped into his and found them surprisingly comfortable. Then someone brought him a pair of boots and took away his shoes and the rest of his clothing.

Until now he had not thought of himself as a prisoner or slave, but looking down at the baggy coveralls and his new boots, the realization suddenly hit home.

He was a slave destined to work in the mines on an alien planet.

A prisoner without any hope of ever escaping his fate.

No! He did not accept that! Somehow he would find a way to escape.

Two of the black-clad guards looked at him. Then they came closer and one of them grabbed his arm, while the other one grabbed Feleena. They were escorted to a teardrop-shaped vehicle and pushed through an opening into its interior.

The vehicle lifted into the air with Feleena and him the only passengers besides their two guards of which one piloted the craft.

Stark watched the clouds through the front windshield. Below them, he could see the tops of the jungle plants rushing by. Then he looked at Feleena. "Is this planet populated at all?" he whispered.

She gave him a questioning look. "No. At least not by civilized societies."

"Is it possible to survive in the jungle?"

She shrugged. "If you can escape the large meat eaters and if you want to fight for your life every day you can survive. Why do you ask?"

He didn't answer. Without thinking, he rose from his seat. Two steps took him to the front of the craft. Putting all of his weight behind it, he brought both of his fists down hard on the neck of the guard in the co-pilot's seat. The guard collapsed without a sound. The pilot reacted before Stark could give him his full attention. With superhuman speed, he slid out of his seat and threw himself at Stark, knocking him into the wall.

He smashed a hard fist into Stark's chest, followed it with another one against the side of Stark's head. Stark locked his hands behind the guard's shiny skull, pulled it down and brought up his knee. He registered with grim satisfaction when he connected with his opponent's face.

There was not much room to move in the confines of the cabin, which might have been in Stark's favor. The guard was strong and fast. He grabbed Stark's shoulders and pressed him against the cabin wall, staring at him with black glittering eyes.

Stark kicked him between the legs with all the strength he could muster and managed to push his opponent back. They both fell onto the front seats and ended up on top of the control board with Stark on top. Lifting his fist, he was ready to smash it into the guard's face, when he noticed that the guard lay limp underneath him.

Then he saw the blood oozing out of his opponent's head and realized that he must have hit it against the hard metal of the console. Judging by the slack face and open eyes Stark knew that the guard was dead.

A loud whining sound filled the cabin and the craft began to wobble. He tried to move the guard but couldn't get a grip on him as he slipped between the seat and the control panel.

All he could do was to hang on tight as the craft lost altitude and sped across the treetops. The whining sound increased; something scraped along the underside of the aircraft and Stark suddenly felt the impact. His body was flung against the windshield, where he lay stunned for a moment.

Someone shook his shoulders. He heard a voice.

"David, come on. We have to get out."

The voice sounded urgent. Then he realized where he was. Groaning, he crawled away from the tight spot he lay in. When he looked, he saw the two guards crushed between the front seats and the console.

"Come on, David."

He stared into Feleena's concerned face. A small streak of blood trickled down her cheek, but otherwise she seemed unhurt.

He managed to stand up swaying. The door to the craft stood open. He inhaled the hot, humid air that rushed into the cabin. Feleena pulled him toward the exit and pushed him outside. His boots sank into the swampy soil, and he moved away from the downed craft.

"Are you all right, David?"

"I think so, except for that rushing in my ears and my hurting head. I must have knocked it against the hard plastic of the windshield when the aircraft hit bottom. How about you? There is blood on your face."

"I'm fine. It's just a scratch." She grabbed his arm. "Let's get away from here as fast as we can. They'll come looking for the ship and us."

He stumbled beside her through the thick vegetation. His boots made sucking sounds as he dragged them through the waterlogged jungle floor. It didn't take long before his clothes were plastered against his skin. When he looked at Feleena he noticed that she had opened the front of her coveralls. Her creamy breasts were slick with sweat. Any other time he would have found it sexually stimulating, but now it only made him aware of his own discomfort.

The vegetation grew thick in places and some of the plants had sharp thorns that ripped the material of their coveralls. Stark's skin stung from cuts where the thorns had left painful slashes.

They followed a narrow trail frequented by some animals. He had no idea where they would end up but it didn't matter, as long as they got far away from the crash site.

"Will they be able to track us?" he asked.

Feleena shook her head. "No, we've been lucky. They didn't collar us. That's a good thing in many ways. The collars can be tracked. They can also deliver painful shocks." She spoke in short sentences interrupted by small gasps as she drew in the hot humid air. When she stumbled, Stark caught her.

"I'm tired." She held on to his arm. "Can we rest for a while?"

He nodded. "Good idea." Leaning against the thick trunk of a tree, he realized suddenly how exhausted he was. He wiped the sweat from his forehead with one grimy hand. "I can't remember the last time I had a good night's rest," he said. Looking up, he tried to see the sky through the thick canopy of green vegetation.

"What is it, David?"

"Nothing." He chuckled. "Hard to believe I'm on another planet. This jungle isn't much different from the one where I was nearly killed so many years ago." He looked into her face and into her strange cat-like eyes. "That's where I met you for the first time. Who are you, Feleena? Or maybe I should ask *what are you*?"

She kept staring at him. "My people come from another solar system. I'm a stranger to this planet as much as you are, but I've been a slave for a long time. All of my people are slaves, like most of the denizens of this part of the Galaxy."

"Slaves to whom?"

"The Almighty Kaloor."

"What did you do on Earth?"

"Looking for you?"

"Why?"

She smiled. "You are full of questions. I needed to find you. I can't explain why, not yet." Her face turned serious. "It is for your own protection that you know as little as possible."

He shook his head. "I don't understand. You were looking for me this time, but what did you and those old men do in the Brazilian jungle when I met you for the first time?"

"We were hiding. When you were brought to us we were elated because we recognized you for what you were, at least we thought we did. Now I'm not so certain anymore."

"You are talking in riddles, Feleena. "What could you possibly want from me?"

"Your help to free us from slavery."

He laughed. "I am an Earthman, a human. Technologically we are so far behind the rest of the Galaxy that we might as well hide in the jungle forever hoping we will never be found by anyone."

Her smile was sad when she looked at him. "You have been found, David. There is no place to hide."

"Tell me more about this Kaloor, your master and god."

"We know he is not a god, David, but he has god-like powers."

"He looked so vulnerable inside his bubble; so helpless."

Feleena lifted her gaze to the sky and sighed. Then she chuckled softly. "He seems helpless, doesn't he? That's what we thought when he we welcomed him and the others of his race with open arms."

"There are more of his kind?" Stark asked astonished. "I was under the impression he was the only one, some kind of mutation, a freak."

"Not a freak. We don't know where they came from. One day their ship arrived in our solar system. When the first one of them floated out of the ship in his transparent globe, we didn't know that our new masters had arrived. Had we known we would have blasted their ship into the next dimension instead of given it permission to land on our planet." She shrugged. "There is only one consolation. We were not the only race duped by their apparent defenselessness."

"The Melkos, those white-faced devils. What are they?"

"They are artificial, soulless creations without feelings and compassion. They are Kaloor's soldiers."

"You said they can read minds?"

She nodded. "You can't hide anything from them. They know your thoughts."

"Why didn't the guard in the ship read my thoughts before I attacked him?"

Her strange eyes studied him silently. "I can't tell you. Perhaps he did but didn't believe you would carry it through." She touched his hand and rose. "Come, we must go on. I want to get as far away from the wrecked ship as is possible."

Stark was still tired, but he agreed. They had to move on. The temperature must have risen and the humidity increased. His wet coveralls clung to his body. He'd like to remove them but knew he needed them for protection against the sharp thorns. His sweating feet ached inside his wet boots, and he could feel blisters forming on his soles. He hadn't walked this much for a long time.

The ground was soggy and made it difficult to walk on. They were still following the trail that wound its way through the thick underbrush. The annoying rushing sound in Stark's head had finally disappeared. His head still hurt, but he could live with that for a while. When he heard a noise that sounded liked gurgling of water, he feared for a fleeting moment that the rushing sound had come back, but then he realized it was actually water he heard.

"We must be close to a creek," he said, suddenly aware of his thirst.

The trail ended in a small clearing. Feleena let out a cry of delight when she saw the pond. There was an outcropping of rocks on the other side with a waterfall that splashed bubbling water into the pond.

Stark laughed when he saw her childish display, as she ran toward the pond and knelt down to scoop out a handful of water. He followed her more slowly, scanning the area for threats. Water meant animals, and there was a good chance some dangerous animals could be hanging around the pond, waiting for prey.

When he didn't see anything that might pose a threat, he dropped to his knees and put his hands into the water. It felt cool and he splashed some into his perspiring face, relishing the feeling of pure pleasure it sent through his tired body. Then he bent to drink from the cool liquid. He didn't drink much, just enough to quench his thirst.

"Be careful," he warned Feleena. "You don't want to get sick."

She laughed and threw a handful of water at him. "Right now I don't care. I've never tasted anything this good." She rose and pushed the top of her coveralls down, exposing her breasts.

He stared as they tumbled into the open, remembering their small size the first time he had seen them. He watched as she kicked off her boots and stripped off the coveralls, admiring the lovely shape of her body.

She noticed his eyes and smiled. "Aren't you getting undressed?" she asked. "I'm going to take a dip in the water."

Again, he looked around, not certain if it was a good idea to enter the pond. Who knew what might lurk under the surface. *Grimy, aching feet, and itchy skin; a bath would not be a bad thing.* Then he shrugged and began to remove his own boots and coveralls. He felt grimy, his feet hurt, and his skin itched. A bath would not be bad thing.

Feleena emitted a cry of joy before she plunged into the water and disappeared into its crystal clear depth. He could see her nude body clearly as she swam toward the middle of the pond, like a nymph returning back to her natural element. She surfaced after a short moment and waved to him. "It is wonderful," she cried. "Come on in."

Throwing another look around, he dove in and swam toward her, enjoying the cool water as it soothed the aches of his body.

Laughing happily, she submerged her head and waited under water for him to reach her. Blowing water, she rose in front of him. She clung to him, pressing her soft breasts against his chest. Her hand went between them and moved down to search for his penis. As she found him, she curled her fingers around it and stroked him gently.

"I've thought about you a lot," she whispered. "You were the first one; you took my virginity. They say you never forget the first one, and I never did."

Treading water, he took her face between his hands and kissed her gently. She returned his kiss with great passion and he could feel his penis swell inside the confines of her hand.

They broke apart, gasping for air. She laughed and pulled on his hard mast. "I believe your mighty weapon is ready to be plunged into a warm sheath."

He pulled her to him again and looked into her strange eyes. "Do you have one in mind?" he asked.

She nodded. "Let's swim back to land and I'll show you."

Slipping from his embrace, she swam back to shore with powerful strokes. He followed her but couldn't catch her. She pulled herself onto the sandy shore and rolled onto her back, her legs spread.

Climbing on land, he stood, looking down at her. "You are so beautiful," he said. "You've been haunting my dreams. I've tried to forget what happened in the jungle, but found it impossible to do."

He dropped between her spread thighs and lay on top of her. Her arms went around his broad back and pulled him into a tight embrace. Capturing his hard penis with the soft labia of her pussy, she pushed up against him. He slid easily into her. She moaned deeply as the moist, warm walls of her sheath molded around his mast and writhed under him.

"I am so happy to be with you," she whispered. "The night in the motel bonded us forever. I hope we never have to part again."

He chuckled and put his hands around her moving hips. With powerful strokes, he moved between her clutching thighs, plunging his swollen penis into her demanding pussy. It didn't take long before she whimpered and doused him with her warm discharge, clinging to him until her orgasm subsided.

Then she began slamming her body against his until another orgasm shook her body. She was strong and took his weight, even though he tried to support his body on his arms.

As tired as he had been, the swim in the cool water had refreshed him and given him new energy. He needed all of that newfound energy to keep up with Feleena. She moved with the ferocity of a wild beast underneath him, her liquid vagina displaying a life of its own as the soft walls rippled the length of his plunging penis.

"Come inside me," she cried out suddenly. "I am ready to receive your gift of passion."

He didn't need any encouragement. His own need had been building up and he felt the sparks that would end in a powerful explosion rising to the surface like a roaring hurricane. He clasped her to him and let it happen. His penis pulsed with every mind-blowing throb as the fruit of his labor jetted out of him into her hungrily sucking vessel.

She whimpered and thrashed in his strong arms, as she accepted his offering, pounding her hips against his in an effort to take him deeper into her. His fingers dug into her quivering buttocks as he kept her from moving erratically. The hot walls of her pulsating vagina squeezed his pumping penis with a powerful grip and held him prisoner until she had swallowed the last drop.

He sank into her arms and lay on top of her soft body, breathing hard. Relaxing her thighs, she sighed and cradled his face between her breasts. "I've needed this for a long time," she whispered, stroking his back with gentle fingers.

"So have I," he murmured. "I just didn't know it." He kissed her soft nipples, took them into his mouth and suckled on them. Then he licked her satiny skin, put his tongue into the hollow of her throat. When his mouth moved along her neck, he became aware of the pulse in her vein and kissed it gently. A strong desire to pierce her skin with his teeth and drink the warm blood from her pulsing vein seemed nearly overwhelming.

He felt her stiffen in his arms. When he lifted his head to look into her face, he saw her eyes wide open in terror as she stared past him.

"What is it?" he asked. "Am I hurting you?"

She didn't answer, just kept staring at something above them.

He turned his head and froze.

The creature that stood beside them was tall, massive, and green. It stared down at them out of bulging eyes set above a flat nose in a brutish face covered with tiny scales. The gaping mouth was filled with small but sharp teeth.

Its long fingers were clamped around a spear, aimed at Stark's back.

Chapter Four

Stark didn't move not knowing what to expect. The spear tip nearly touched his skin and any quick movement would only end up with it buried in his back. He noticed that the creature was not alone. Behind it stood at least a dozen, maybe more. All of them were armed with long spears. Even if he did have a weapon, he knew that he was disadvantaged. Trapped between the thighs of a woman with his penis still inside her vagina was not a position to be in when confronted by an enemy.

"Don't move," Feleena whispered needlessly.

"I have no such intentions," he murmured.

The creature above him uttered a deep-throated cry. Then it kicked him in the side with a hard, clawed foot. He let out an involuntary shout and rolled off Feleena despite his fears that he might be attacked. He hated to leave her vulnerable, as she lay unprotected on her back looking up at the creature, her thighs still open, her genitalia exposed, but the creature ignored her.

Stepping over her, it advanced toward Stark, as he crouched on the ground, staring at the strange being that might run its spear through him within the next few moments.

However, his fears proved unfounded. With a gesture, the creature told him to get up. Cautiously, he rose to his feet and stood wide legged, his eyes watching warily, waiting for the brute's next move.

Studying his opponent, he noted the savage face but didn't let that fool him. This was not a dumb animal, even though he didn't see any clothes. The green body was covered with thick scales and shiny plates, like armor. He could see bulging muscles under the plates. The long thighs were thick and strong, with muscular legs and large feet. The toes were tipped with sharp, wicked claws that could easily rip open a man's torso with one swipe.

Frogs, he thought. They look like giant frogs.

He smiled, hoping it would communicate friendliness and non-violence. "I am unarmed," he said, feeling foolish. As naked as he was, anyone could see that he didn't hide any weapons. "We mean you no harm," he added, still smiling and spreading his arms in a gesture of good will.

The *Frog-man* stared at him with his bulging eyes. Stark couldn't tell if his words and stance conveyed his intended message. He glanced at Feleena. Seeing the terror in her eyes and face, he became angry…at himself for having been so careless and angry at the creatures who dared to threaten them.

Feleena looked at him. She must have seen it in his eyes and posture that he intended to take a stand against his opponent. "Don't do anything foolish, David," she begged. "They won't harm us."

"What do they want from us?" he asked.

32

"No more than I've been giving for a long time."

"What do you mean?"

"These are our new masters, David. We've been captured. We'll be their slaves."

"I won't be anyone's slave," he said defiantly.

She smiled bravely. "If you want us to live, you will let them take you. If you resist, they will kill you…and me. Do you want that?"

"No." He straightened and let out a loud sigh. "This situation will only be temporarily until I can figure something out," he promised.

"I know," she said.

He didn't resist when they wrapped him with thin cords and hung him from a long pole carried by two Frogmen on their wide shoulders. He hung suspended like a gutted deer and hoped that he was not destined to be their next meal.

The Frogmen followed the same trail he and Feleena had used and he realized that eventually, had they walked on, they would have ended up wherever their captors were taking them.

Finally, they entered another clearing. This one was large and he knew they had arrived in the village of the Frog people. A number of huts were placed in a huge circle, leaving the inside clear and free of obstacles. His carriers dumped him unceremoniously in the middle of the cleared area. Feleena suffered the same fate.

Stark tried to roll onto his side to get a better view of his surroundings. He heard croaking and trumpeting from many voices and saw the inhabitants of the village congregating around them and the warriors who had brought them.

He saw beings of different sizes. Some of them were quite small, and he knew these were the children. He also saw the females and was surprised that they didn't look as ugly and savage as the males. Their noses were more defined and their mouths not as large. Had it not been for the protruding eyes they could have almost passed for human. They had breasts and nicely formed bodies, covered by fine, green scales. Their long legs were slender with muscular thighs and their clawed feet smaller and thinner.

The younger ones tried to touch the captives but a few kicks kept them at bay.

Two of the warriors who had brought them picked up Feleena again and began walking away with her.

"David," she called, her voice desperate and afraid. "Don't let them hurt me."

He struggled with his bonds, but realized he could do nothing to help her. Angry and helpless he watched as they disappeared with her in the jungle.

One of the Frogmen bent over him and cut away the strands with a blade made from stone. When the pieces of rope fell off, he rose to his feet and rubbed his arms and legs to bring the circulation back into them. He stared defiantly at the crowd who watched him with their expressionless faces, wondering what they thought about him.

Two of his captors motioned with their hands. He knew they wanted him to come with them and he walked between them as they headed for another trail that led away from the village.

He thought of escaping but gave up that notion. Where would he go? And what about Feleena? He couldn't abandon her.

They didn't walk far until they came to the end of the path. Stark stared with astonishment at the expanse of water stretching out in front of him. Small waves rippled across a huge lake that seemed to go on forever.

They walked along the sandy shore for a while, heading for a destination unknown to Stark. When they rounded a giant, red boulder, he stopped involuntarily and let out a sound of surprise.

A vast lagoon lay ahead of them. Huge rocks covered much of the shore. Gurgling water spilled across the rocks, churning up the surface of the lagoon. A thick mist hung in the air, creating an eerie setting, like a scene from a horror play.

The water seemed to bubble gently, as if it were boiling. Stark bent and carefully put his hand into the water, expecting it to be hot, but he found it only comfortably warm.

One of the Frogmen gave him a push, indicating for Stark to move. With a shrug, he walked on. When he looked back, he noticed his escort wasn't following him. After watching him for a short time, they turned and walked back the way they had come.

Stark didn't know where he was supposed to go but kept on walking along a narrow trail winding between giant boulders. On his right the jungle formed a thick barrier. Had he entertained any thoughts of escaping into the apparent safety of the jungle, he may have taken a chance, but his fear for Feleena's well-being didn't allow such thoughts.

He wondered why they had brought him to this place. He didn't believe that he was in any danger. Everything seemed so peaceful. The gurgling of water splashing into the lagoon created a feeling of serenity. The setting sun threw long shadows. Its rays lit up the mist in rainbow colors.

He stopped when he heard what seemed like music. Listening, he realized it was the sound of strings. And then he heard someone singing. The voice was definitely human, male, and the melody quite familiar, but not the words.

Where the golden sun shines in the sky
Where the wind lifts my spirit high
I left the one who has my heart
On Earth forever will she it guard

Hastening his steps, Stark walked on. When he rounded the next boulder, he saw the naked back of a wide-shouldered man sitting on a rock. He sat facing the lagoon; his hair was long and unkempt. Stark saw that the man held an instrument that resembled a guitar. Beside him, lay a number of long spears.

He played the instrument with great skill and sang with a descent baritone. There was no doubt in Stark's mind that the stranger was an Earthman. With a shout of joy he nearly ran toward the man.

When he stepped in front of the stranger, his assumption proved correct. The man looked up and stared at Stark. His eyes widened and he stopped playing.

"Where do you come from?" he stammered. Putting down his musical instrument, he rose. "Are you from Earth? Can you understand me?"

Stark nodded. "Yes to both questions," he said.

The man rushed toward him, and before Stark could say anything else, the stranger hugged him with crushing force. "I am so glad to see you," he said with a choked voice. Tears rolled down his face and collected in his scraggly beard. "I haven't seen another human for a long time." Letting go of Stark, he stepped back. "You are human, aren't you?"

Stark chuckled. "Yes again. Why do you ask?"

"Because I am not sure of anything anymore. Ever since I got captured by those white-faced devils I've seen things I never knew existed."

"Who are you?" Stark asked.

"My name is Kenneth Borton."

"Kenneth Borton?" Stark repeated. "Are you by any chance *Captain* Kenneth Borton?"

The man smiled. "The very same one. I assume you know who I am?"

"Who doesn't know Captain Kenneth Borton?" Stark studied the man. His large frame was covered with corded muscles, but his bearded face looked haggard. He was eight years older than the last time Stark had seen him. He and millions of other people who had watched the first manned mission to Mars. He had followed the news as it reported the flight of the spaceship. It was a momentous undertaking in the history of mankind. Everybody took an interest. After three months into the journey, the reports stopped coming. It seemed the ship had disappeared into nowhere.

"What happened?" he asked.

Borton sighed. "We never made it to Mars. Our great ship was captured by aliens. We were brutally forced to face the fact that we weren't the only ones in the Galaxy, and that it was not a friendly place. The conquest of space by the human race was nothing but an impossible dream. Our first contact with an extraterrestrial race didn't happen the way we had envisioned. We became prisoners and slaves with no hope of ever seeing our home planet again."

Stark made a face. "I never really thought much about aliens from outer space. That was the stuff of Science Fiction novels and movies. Only writers and dreamers filled their heads with that."

Borton smiled. "And scientists."

35

"Those too, I guess." Stark shook his head in disgust. "I was treated like a primitive savage, like an animal. Look at me." He made a gesture. "I am naked and caked with mud. Those *Frogmen* carried me through the jungle hanging from a pole like a trophy animal ready to be gutted and hung over a fire."

Borton laughed, obviously amused by Stark's words. "You call them *Frogmen*. I just call them *Frogs*, even though they don't have much in common with the frogs on Earth. And don't worry about being naked. As you can see so am I. The Frogs don't wear clothes either."

"What happened to the rest of the crew?"

Borton shrugged. "I have no idea where Dr. Solder is right now. He was captured again when we made our escape from the mine we slaved in. Dr. Malokov was killed. I was the only one who got away." He laughed hoarsely. "Only to be taken prisoner by the Frogs. I've been their captive ever since. Freedom is not something that exists in the Galaxy we live in…" He stopped talking and whirled.

A few steps took him to the rock he'd been sitting on. He bent and grabbed two spears.

Stark heard a sound above him, like the sound of great flapping wings. When he looked up, he saw a creature that looked much like a giant lizard with a pair of leathery wings. It had a long neck and a beak like a bird. A sack hung from the giant beak.

Borton threw Stark one of the spears. "Here. The Edder is going to attack any moment. Be ready."

Stark held the spear awkwardly. He had never used a primitive weapon like this. He was trained in the use of machine guns, rifles and handguns. He was quite efficient with a composite bow but not in throwing a spear.

As if to confirm Borton's words, the Edder folded its leathery wings and shot like a missile toward the ground.

Stark lifted his spear, but the giant lizard ignored the two humans. Instead it aimed for something in the water. Its great wings opened as it neared the surface and its beak opened to scoop up something Stark couldn't see. Before the Edder reached the water, Borton threw his spear. The tip buried itself in the exposed wide chest.

With a shrill cry, and beating its giant wings, the Edder tried to lift into the air, but it clearly was mortally wounded. It hit the water, its wings flapping frantically. Disappearing under the churning surface, it let out one more desperate cry, its broad head above water. Then it vanished completely. The water boiled for a while at the spot where the Edder had sunk beneath the surface.

Stark and Borton watched without saying anything until it was quiet again.

"What the hell was that all about?" Stark asked.

Borton grinned. "You were just initiated into our job."

"What do you mean by our job? I don't think I understand."

"Take a look into the water."

Stark walked to the water's edge and peered into the clear liquid.

"What do you see?" Borton asked.

"I see something moving in there. Looks like a bunch of giant tadpoles."

"Quite an accurate description; those are the children of the Frogs. We are their keepers. You might say we are the babysitters."

Stark gave him a questioning look. "We are talking about the Frog people here?"

Borton nodded.

"Are you telling me they lay eggs? How can that be? I saw their young and I saw the females. They have breasts. I don't know too much about biology, but I always assumed only mammals have breasts. They need them to suckle their young."

"You are correct. Forget everything you learned in School. This is an alien planet. Things are different here. The Frogs have a social structure and they are actually quite intelligent. They don't have families. The males and females couple at random. When a female becomes pregnant and her time comes to deliver, she will go down to the lake and lay her eggs into the water."

Borton walked over to his rock and sat down. "The eggs hatch and the tadpoles swim out to sea where they grow. When they reach a certain size they come back to this lagoon. Not many come back, as you can well imagine. There are plenty of dangers in the lake to prevent that from happening. Even the lagoon is not a safe haven. Only a few survive. Here in the lagoon is where the survivors start to change and acquire their intelligence."

He pointed to the middle of the lagoon. "Do you see the little bubbles?"

Stark followed his pointing finger and nodded.

"The bottom of the lake is covered with radioactive rock. It warms the water. The tadpoles search out this warm water and the steady radioactivity mutates them. They change and become intelligent. The majority of them doesn't survive this process, and the ones who do are still in danger. They are eaten by their many enemies. The Edder is only one of them. Our job is to save as many of them as is possible, but we can only do so much. For instance, we can't keep them from eating each other."

He chuckled when he saw Stark's astonished look. "Yes, they are cannibals. But once they crawl on land even this danger has passed." He laughed. "Don't worry, the Frogs are not cannibals. In fact, they won't eat other intelligent beings. We are quite safe."

"Well, that's a relief," Stark said.

"At the land stage of their development they have changed into mammals. Now the pregnant females take over and let them suckle on their breasts until they outgrow their need for milk and can start eating on their own."

"How large are they when they crawl on land?" Stark asked.

"As large as a human baby, but they grow much faster than humans. In about a year they reach the size of a five year old and are on their own. The young are kept in their own corral where they are taught by the elder Frogs."

Stark folded his legs under him and sat on the warm sand. Staring at the great red ball of the setting sun, its light diffused by the mist, he sighed and murmured, "Frogs…intelligent frogs. Who would have thought?"

Chapter Five

He sensed the presence of someone standing in the opening of the hut he and Borton shared. Rising from his half-sleep, he stared at the silhouette of the creature. "What do you want?" His voice came out in a croak that could have competed with the sounds the Frogs made.

The Frog said something in his own language. Stark didn't understand but he guessed that he was supposed to come with the scaly humanoid. He crawled into the open and gave Borton, who was sitting on his rock, a questioning look. "Where is he taking me?"

Borton chuckled softly. "You will be introduced to T'Phira today."

"Who is T'Phira?"

"She is the Frog queen, the Golden Goddess." Borton turned away and looked across the misty lagoon. "Good luck."

Stark followed the frogman with mixed emotions. "The Golden Goddess," he murmured. "I wonder what she wants from me."

They followed the shoreline of the lake for a while. Then they took a path that led into the jungle. They walked for a long time and when Stark was beginning to wonder where they were heading, the path ended and he looked across a large valley. In the distance, he spotted a structure which he recognized as a wall built from tall timber.

As they neared the wall, he saw a gate guarded by two Frogs armed with spears. They barred the entry to the enclosure behind them, but Stark's companion barked a command and they stepped aside to let them pass.

Stark suppressed a sound of surprise when he stepped into the enclosure. It was like stepping into another world.

Tall, colorful flowers and plants grew everywhere. Narrow paths snaked their way through them, leading to places where Stark could only guess. He and his guard walked on a wide gravel path toward a building that loomed ahead of them. It presented Stark with another surprise. This was not a simple, primitive hut. It could only be described as a palace.

The entrance to the building stood open. It was guarded by two Frogs who threw curious glances at Stark as he passed them, but they didn't make any moves to keep him from entering the interior of the building.

Huge pillars supported a roof made from stone. The walls were covered with colorful drawings. Large openings let in the light, but Stark noticed that they could be closed by curtains made from bamboo-like sticks.

At the end of the room they entered, a slim figure reclined on a bed made from giant shells.

A humanoid figure.

A female humanoid figure.

She was naked. Long, golden hair cascaded from her head, partially covering her breasts. The sun shone through one of the windows and lit up her skin with shimmering colors, but when Stark came closer, he saw that her skin was actually golden.

Her black eyes studied him silently. Then she smiled and broke into silvery laughter. "You seem surprised," she said. She rose and walked up to him. She was almost as tall as he. Her eyes glittered as she looked at him with an amused smile on her beautiful face. "What did you expect to find?"

He stared into her face, covered with tiny, golden scales, as was the rest of her shapely body. Her lips and nose were human. Even her eyes did not appear alien, if one overlooked the fact that her eyeballs were completely black.

Her arms and legs didn't end in claws but in slim toes and fingers.

"I did not expect a human-looking woman," he admitted.

"I am T'Phira," she said proudly.

"You speak my language," he said.

"I speak many. I have a gift for languages." She grabbed his arm and pulled him with her. "Come, sit with me."

Her hand felt warm and yet…he shuddered.

She was not human. When he looked, he saw the webbing between her fingers and toes. She was a Frog. How could she look like this?

Hesitating, he sat down beside her on the bed made from shells. T'Phira clapped her hands and spoke a few words in the guttural language of the Frogs. From an entrance behind the bed rushed one of the young female Frogs. She carried two cups and a large container. She filled the two cups with a dark liquid and handed one to T'Phira and the other one to Stark. Then she put the container onto the floor in front of the bed.

She sat down cross-legged on one side and waited patiently until she was needed again.

"Drink," T'Phira said. "You must be thirsty."

Stark held the cup under his nose and sniffed, wondering what she offered him. The liquid looked murky and had a dubious aroma. He took a small sip, swallowing the bitter-sweet fluid. It left a strange aftertaste in the back of his throat.

T'Phira was watching him with an amused expression. She laughed merrily. "You Earthmen are all alike. Borton acted the same way the first time we met, but he learned to appreciate and enjoy the times he spent in my presence." She lowered her long golden lashes and looked at him out of veiled eyes. "You also will find my company desirable. But be warned. I am not easily pleased and quickly grow tired of others. Disappoint me and I will not seek your company again."

She lifted her cup and emptied it. "Come, drink yours." Her eyes studied him across the rim of her cup. "No harm will come to you. That I promise."

40

He followed her example and drained his cup. The liquid ran down his throat like hot fire. It seemed to go right into his veins.

"That's good." She motioned to the Frog girl to refill the cups.

"I'm not sure if I should," Stark said, finding it difficult to formulate the words clearly. It seemed as if a fog had enveloped his brain.

T'Phira sipped from her cup. She reached out and put her hand under Stark's. Then she lifted his cup to his lips. "Do not resist," she whispered with a husky voice. "You are in no danger. Only pleasure awaits you."

He became aware of a strong scent in the air. Then he noticed the red flowers standing beside the bed. The scent seemed to originate from those flowers. He also noticed a faint mist rising from the flowers.

T'Phira saw him looking. "They are the *Flowers of Fertility*. Inhaling their scent loosens your inhibitions and makes you more pliable to suggestions." She offered him her cup. "How do you like the water?" she asked, purring softly.

"That's not water," he said, his word coming out slurred.

She leaned against him and looked into his eyes. "It is special water," she murmured. Then she put her hand behind his head and pulled him close. Her lips touched his. Opening her lips, she pushed her tongue into his mouth. He noted its length as it touched the back of his throat.

He put his arms around her and kissed her hungrily, sucking on her long tongue. Between his legs, his penis had grown and his desire for this alien woman could not be denied. He was beyond caution and self-control.

She broke the kiss and moved her lips down and across his chest, licking his belly with her tongue and fondling his scrotum with gentle fingers. Taking the tip of his penis into her mouth, she ran her tongue around it, teasing him until he was ready to explode. Then she sucked him deep into her. He couldn't hold back any longer and exploded inside her soft mouth. She swallowed his jetting stream and licked him clean.

Looking at him with a lazy expression, she smiled and grazed his penis with her sharp teeth. He was still stiff and his desire still strong.

She lay back on the bed and pulled him on top of her. Her legs opened wide and he slid between her strong thighs. As she pressed her supple body against his, her hand snaked down to his penis and her long fingers encircled it. She laughed when she discovered him still hard and rubbed her genitalia over his swollen member. She was wet and slippery and when he found her opening, he slid into her with ease.

She moaned into his ear as she welcomed his entry into her vessel and rotated her lower body in slow circles. A deep groan escaped his lips as she squeezed his swollen penis with the soft walls of her vagina.

He grabbed her moving buttocks and held her still while he pushed deep into her with every powerful thrust. Her cries of pleasure rang through the room and she raked his back with her fingers as she bucked beneath him.

In one of her calm moments, she gasped, "Let me be on top."

He pulled out of her and lay on his back. She straddled him and hovered above his straining penis. He watched as her thick, hairless labia stretched over the head of his swollen member. Slowly, she sank into his lap and took him back into her hot sheath of flesh. Lifting her arms above her head, she rode him with wild abandon. Her hips churned with ever increasing movements as she pumped her hot vagina over his hard penis. He reached up to take her solid breasts into his hands and dug his fingers into their soft tissue. The pleasure she created inside him was incredible. He couldn't get enough of her. Never before had a woman given him such level of satisfaction and joy.

He swam in a sea of happiness and time stood still, but there came the moment when he couldn't go on any longer. As waves of pleasure rushed through his body, he became aware of the strong scent from the *Flowers of Fertility*. He saw the Frog girl standing beside them. She threw red petals on top of his chest and belly. He shouted with joy and exploded inside T'Phira's milking sheath, his hands squeezing her taut breasts.

She clamped down hard and sat quivering in his lap, her black eyes large and her gaze locked with his. Her lips parted and her tongue darted between her white teeth. A soft hissing sound escaped her mouth as the enflamed walls of her tightening sex-organ sucked him dry.

Then she let out a sigh of contentment and collapsed on top of him. Her breasts flattened against his chest. He could feel the hard nipples as she lay on top of him, her breath coming in great gasps.

"You did not disappoint," she said after a while. Then she laughed and wiggled her bottom. "You are still hard inside me. I don't remember Borton being this virile?"

He grinned and put his hands around her undulating hips. "It must be the water you gave me to drink and those flowers."

"Yes, they would be of great assistance. But they are useless if the male does not have stamina…like you." She gasped and moved her buttocks up and down. She said something in the language of the Frogs. The young female who still stood beside them, bent and picked up one of the cups and offered the liquid to Stark, who drank every drop.

He felt the liquid going down his throat. Within moments, the fire in his loins burned hot and he put his arms around T'Phira, turning her onto her back. Then he pumped between her clutching thighs with renewed vigor. He took a long time until he filled her vessel again and he cried out hoarsely when he felt his sperm shooting into her.

Exhausted, he fell asleep in her arms.

* * * *

The difference between a dream and reality is the dreamer believes what he is experiencing is real, but the man who is awake knows the world he lives in is real.

At least he thinks he knows…until waking with the realization he was only dreaming and wondering if what is remembered of the dream was real.

Time has no meaning in the world of dreams. There is no past and no future, only the present…

…He floated between the worlds, watched a planet drift by as it turned slowly around its axis, creating day and night for the creatures that populated it. Reaching out with a mental finger, he touched it, followed it on its path around its primary sun.

Then he lost the connection and drifted back into the dark void.

He was alone.

"Who am I?" He couldn't remember.

After drifting for a long time he became aware of another mind, felt the tentative touch as it tried to make contact with him.

He saw a face in the mist that surrounded him.

"Who are you?" he asked, staring into the mist. The face seemed to hover nearby but he sensed it was far away. He sent out a searching thought tendril, touched the other mind, but only for a moment then it slipped from his grasp. "Stay," he called. "Don't leave."

"I can't," the voice whispered.

"Then let me come to you."

"No."

"Can you tell me who I am?"

"You will remember. You must go back." The voice faded away.

"I remember pain. I don't want to go back."

Suddenly he felt the comforting touch of a mind so strong it nearly overwhelmed him, but he didn't feel any threat, only love and reassurance. "Do not be afraid to live," the voice said. "You will not be alone. I will be with you and lend you strength when you are in need."

A feeling of happiness and calm overcame him, filled his whole being. He knew things he shouldn't have known, remembered experiences he couldn't have had, but he accepted them as his own.

He needed to go back to his battered body. It would heal, of that he was sure now…

* * * *

He sat up and stared at the naked woman beside him, momentarily confused. Her skin shimmered golden in the light that fell through one of the windows. Her long golden hair covered part of her face, but he knew she was different from him.

"Where am I?" he murmured. He looked at the young Frog girl who sat beside the bed, her legs crossed in front of her. She watched him with her bulging eyes, her face without expression.

Memory came back with a sudden rush.

T'Phira's lids fluttered open and she stirred. Her hand reached up to touch his chest. Smiling, she put her arms around his neck and pulled herself up. "Sleep well?" she asked, yawning.

"Maybe too well," he said. "My sleep was disturbed by strange dreams."

She laughed. "That is the aftereffect of the Flowers. They open your mind and let you travel through the many worlds of your dreams. Sometimes you remember them." She stretched her lithe body languidly. Her ample breasts glistened with golden fire and he put his hand on one.

She brushed his hand away with an impatient gesture. "Not now," she said, sliding from the bed. "Today the young ones will climb on land. We will celebrate tonight."

She clapped her hands. One of the Frog-males, who stood waiting against a wall, came closer. T'Phira pointed at Stark and spoke a few words in the language of the Frogs. Then she turned back to Stark. "Go with him. He will take you back."

Her voice sounded cold and distant, and Stark knew he had been dismissed. He followed his guard out of the palace, down the wide grave path between the flowers. When they reached the gate that surrounded the palace grounds, he froze and stared at the figure standing beside the gate. A cape hung from wide shoulders and Stark had an uncomfortable feeling in the pit of his stomach.

The caped figure turned and when Stark saw the white, expressionless face, he wondered if he should try to escape down one of the narrow paths. He stood waiting, but the Melkos only threw a quick glance at him as he passed by.

Stark's guard gave him a push and uttered a few syllables in his guttural language. He stumbled on, wondering what the Melkos wanted here at the palace.

I thought they could read minds. Why couldn't he read mine?

His thoughts in turmoil, he walked beside the Frog, back to the place by the beach where Borton was busy guarding the tadpoles.

Chapter Six

Stark watched the Edder circling above the lagoon and tightened his grip on the spear. When he looked at Borton, he saw the other man also watched the giant reptile.

"We have to make certain the overgrown lizard doesn't get a chance to make a meal out of the young Frogs. They'll be climbing on land soon." He eyed the bubbling water of the lagoon warily.

Both men turned and looked at the crowd of Frogs who suddenly appeared around the giant boulder. Stark spotted T'Phira, the Golden Goddess. She sat on a contraption made from reeds, carried on the shoulders of four Frog males.

They put her down in the sand and stood behind her.

A few young Frogs ran around, squealing as they chased each other. Stark couldn't help but compare them with human children, who would act the same way on a day by the beach.

The older Frogs sat cross-legged in the sand, watching the lagoon. He saw a number of the males with spears. Some of them held large nets in their clawed hands.

Excited shouts from a few of the watching Frogs made him turn around to look at the water. A green head appeared on the surface. He saw the large mouth, as the little creature came up gasping for breath.

Slowly, the green creature swam toward shore and climbed out of the water on shaky legs.

"Watch out," Borton shouted, and Stark turned his attention toward the sky.

The Edder had decided that it was time to join the party. With wings laid against its scaly body, it swooped down, its target obviously the little Frog who stood looking around with its large, protruding eyes.

Stark gripped his spear with both hands and ran toward the little creature, stood above it with his spear aiming into the sky. Borton joined him momentarily, and both men tried to keep the new arrival safe, which was no easy task because it kept wandering along the water's edge.

The Edder came closer, like a dive-bombing plane, obviously not daunted by the presence of the two men, and Stark planted the end of the long spear into the sand to absorb the shock when the reptile hit.

Before it slammed into the ground, the Edder opened its giant wings and, flapping furiously, it landed on the ground in front of the men. With open beak, it advanced, trying to get at the small, squeaking green creature tumbling around in the sand.

Stark ran at it with his spear held low, aiming for the underside of the long neck. He knew that it was one of the vulnerable spots on the giant lizard. Feeling the spear go in, he held on as the Edder tried to dislodge it. Screaming defiantly, the huge creature snapped at Stark, who jumped back but lost his grip on the spear in the process.

Borton pushed his spear into the Edder's open beak and hung on for dear life as the lizard shook its wide, broad head, hissing and roaring.

The Earthmen would have lost the battle had it not been for the Frog warriors who came to their aid. Uttering loud, gurgling sounds, they attacked the Edder with their spears and before long, the giant beast lay dead on the ground, pierced by a dozen spears.

In the meantime, another of the young Frogs had climbed on land and ran around, squeaking loudly. Then another one joined them and then another.

A couple of them began running toward the jungle, but before they reached the edge of the thick growth, two of the Frogs with nets captured them and carried them toward the cheering crowd.

Borton leaned on his spear, which he had pulled out of the Edder's beak and grinned. "This is a momentous event," he said. "Like a national holiday on Earth. Tonight, they'll be celebrating with a barbecue and all the trimmings."

"What are they barbecuing?"

"The Edder, what else?"

"How about us? Are we invited?" Stark said, trying to make a joke.

Borton gave him a long look. His gaze wandered over to the golden woman. "We will be, but I have a feeling it will be you this time, my friend, who will get the special treatment," he said slowly.

"Special treatment?"

"You'll see."

Stark wondered why Borton sounded so mysterious when he said that. He watched as the Frogs tied ropes around the carcass of the dead Edder. At least the beast would not rot on the beach and pollute the air and water, possibly attracting other carnivores and vultures.

"I hope Edder meat tastes good," he said.

"Like chicken," Borton said, grinning. "A bit tough, though."

Squealing sounds from the shore announced the arrival of another hatched Frog, but fortunately, the Edder they had slain, was the only one who had decided to come looking for an easy meal. After seven more hatchlings climbed on shore, the migration ceased and the crowd went back to the village. When evening came, two guards came and indicated Stark and Borton should accompany them.

Nearing the village, Stark could smell roasting meat. The Frogs had lit a huge fire in the center of the open area inside the circle of houses. Pieces of Edder meat were suspended above the fire from huge poles driven into the ground.

The whole village seemed to be assembled around the fire. Some were dancing a grotesque dance in a cleared area.

Stark and Borton joined the ones on the ground and watched the dancers. Stark saw males and females. They didn't dance together but he seemed to recognize a certain pattern as they swirled and danced around each other.

Almost like a mating dance.

A group of Frog warriors came for Stark before he had a chance to try some of the Edder meat.

He walked between them as they headed for the palace. It was dark, but one of the three moons had come up and threw its pale light on the path. Torches attached to the walls lit up the interior of the palace. A few were dispersed throughout the room, secured inside tall vases.

T'Phira reclined on her bed made from shells. She watched him as he approached but didn't give him any signs that might convey familiarity.

She nodded when he stood in front of her. "Earthman, I have chosen you to entertain me at this night of Celebration."

Stark gave her a small bow and smiled. "Whatever it is you have planned for me, I shall not disappoint you, Golden Goddess."

She didn't smile, only looked at him with her black eyes. "I watched you defend our young and I am pleased with your performance. This will be your reward." She waved to one of the Frog girls who came rushing closer. She held a cup between her long fingers and offered it to Stark.

He took it from her and without sniffing at the contents, emptied the cup. Feeling the thick liquid go down his throat, he waited for the fire to rush through his veins. When it came, it seemed to go straight down to his genitals. A strong desire to join the golden woman on her bed and take her into his arms rose up inside him. He fought the urge, knowing it would not be appropriate.

When he looked around, he saw the room filled with Frog people. They watched him with curiosity as if waiting for something to happen. Many of them were young females. As he looked at their naked bodies, he found himself drawn to them. Staring at their nubile breasts, he felt a strong throbbing in his loins.

The scent of the red flowers that stood around the Golden Goddess's bed rose up strong in his nostrils and when he looked down he saw his penis standing like a giant pole below his belly.

The Golden Goddess clapped her hands. Two of the young Frog girls approached Stark and began running their hands across his chest and arms. Their touch was soft and sent electrifying shocks throughout his body.

One of them crouched in front of him and put her hands around his stiff pole. Then she bent forward and caressed the tip with her lips. Running her long tongue around it, she slowly sucked its full length into her mouth. The hot interior of her mouth almost made him want to explode, but he controlled the urge and closed his eyes, enjoying the pleasure she gave him as she worked her tongue and the back of her throat around his hard flesh.

She released him before he climaxed and put her hand on his chest. The other girl pushed on his shoulders. He sank to his knees and stretched out on the floor. Lying on his back, he watched the girl who had sucked him straddle his lower body. Never having given the genitals of the Frog people a closer look before, he was surprised to find that the girl's sex-organ looked like that of a human female. Her pronounced vulva was hairless and smooth.

His gaze wondered up to her breasts. They were well formed, covered with tiny, shimmering scales and not too large, which pleased him, since he had never cared much for women with oversized breasts. He noticed the long, thick nipples and felt the urge to take one of them into his mouth.

The Frog girl lowered herself onto his straining member. He moaned deeply when her long, soft labia closed around his engorged head and watched with anticipation as the length of his penis slowly disappeared inside the Frog girl's hot and satiny sheath.

Her strong thighs allowed her to support her body with ease as she slowly moved up and down. Her black, protruding eyes watched him as she rotated her body above him. A small sound, like a soft whimper escaped her open mouth and she ran her tongue across her thick lips He felt warm liquid running onto his thighs and knew she was experiencing an orgasm.

For a moment she sat quivering in his lap then she lifted up, freeing his penis. Disappointed, he watched her move away. His gaze fell on T'Phira who had been watching with intend. She waved to the girl who knelt beside Stark's head.

The girl straddled him, but with her back toward him. He stared at her round, firm buttocks; saw the thick lips of her vagina below them. She grabbed his penis and guided it between her buttocks. His penis slid easily into her moist vagina and he welcomed the tight, soft walls of her hot sheath. Moving slowly at first, she soon increased the rhythm of her up and down movements.

Before long, her buttocks churned wildly and became a blur. She let out soft little cries at almost regular intervals. He tried desperately to keep from coming but finally he lost the battle. Shouting hoarsely, he clamped his hands around her moving hips and pushed up to bury his pumping penis deep into her. He exploded with powerful bursts, dimly aware of the girl's squealing sounds.

She stopped churning and sat in his lap until he was finished. Then she left him and walked away, her movements sluggish.

Stark's breath came in great gasps as he lay staring at nothing. The tremendous climax experienced left him momentarily weak, but he became aware of his strutting penis. His body was not satisfied and neither was his mind. The desire was still strong inside him.

Someone lifted his head and put a cup against his lips. He drank eagerly, felt the liquid run down his chin and onto his chest. One of the girls bent over him and licked it off with her long tongue. Then she lay on top of him and clamped her thighs around his hard member. Lifting up, she impaled herself on him and took him deep into her hot vagina.

While she moved slowly, her soft breasts resting on his chest, her hands caressed his cheeks and ears. He looked into her black eyes. Even in his muddled state he noticed that her face was delicately formed and her green skin smooth and shiny. He felt like kissing her thick lips and put his hand behind her head. Pulling her close, he kissed her and was surprised when she returned the kiss.

They may not look like us but they are not so much different from us. They have feelings and are quite passionate.

He embraced her and held her young, warm body tightly while she fucked him with slow, steady movements. He took a long to come and when he did, it was with great force and unbelievable pleasure.

She left him and he sat up to look at T'Phira. The Golden Goddess seemed pleased. She smiled and said, "Come and sit with me, Earthman."

He rose and walked over to the bed, feeling somewhat weak.

"Rest," T'Pira said, waiting until he was seated. She took it upon herself to offer him another drink. He accepted it gratefully and let the bittersweet liquid trickle down his parched throat. It seemed to lend him strength almost instantly.

"Sit and watch," she said.

A few of the Frog girls began dancing. Stark watched them with great interest and was surprised at the suppleness and agility the girls displayed. They twisted their slender bodies and jumped with fluid movements into the air. It was like watching a ballet, something he had enjoyed many times on Earth.

"Do you enjoy pain?" T'Phira asked suddenly.

"What?" He was surprised by her unexpected question.

"Do you enjoy pain?" She repeated.

"Not particularly. Why do you ask?"

"There is not much difference between pleasure and pain." Her dark eyes were veiled when she looked at him. "Both can be enjoyed." She leaned over and kissed him on the lips. Without warning, she raked her fingers across his chest, leaving a red welt.

He let out a small yelp when he felt the sudden pain.

She slipped off the bed and stood over him, a whip in her hand. Stepping back, she flicked the tip across his belly. The whip stung just enough to be unpleasant.

Surprised by her action, he sat up. "Why?" he asked.

She laughed. "Because it pleases me," and used the whip again. This time the leash wound around his upper torso. She moved toward him, winding the leash in her hands. Stepping close, her hand went down to his penis and her fingers wrapped around the shaft. They felt hot and he reacted.

Her silvery laughter teased him. Removing the leash from his body, she handed the whip to one of the Frog males standing beside the bed. Then she knelt on the floor, her golden buttocks up. Looking back, she ordered, "Mount me."

He obliged. Kneeling behind her, he put his hard penis between her fleshy buttocks. She pushed back and he slid into her creamy sex-organ. When he began moving in and out of her, he heard the cracking of a whip. A streak of pain burned across his back. He stopped moving but carried on when T'Phira said with a sharp voice, "Don't stop."

With every thrust he made into her, the Frog male laid the whip across his back. After a while he became oblivious to the pain and ignored it. T'Phira bucked in front of him, pumping her hot sheath across his throbbing penis. The lash seemed to come every time she took him deep into her and after a while, he longed for the pain because of the pleasure T'Phira created for him.

"Use your fingers on my back," she panted over her shoulder.

He knew what she wanted. His fingernails left red marks as he raked them across her smooth, golden skin.

"More," she called out. "I want to feel the pain." She let out a loud hissing sound when he drew blood and pushed her buttocks back into his groin. "Yess…yess…that's it!"

He grabbed her long hair with one hand and pulled back her head. She struggled and cried out when his other hand dug into her breast and squeezed her nipple. Her breath came fast and she arched her back. He pounded into her with full force, slamming his hips into her soft buttocks.

Slapping her on one of her buttocks with his flat hand, he let out a moan when the whip was laid across his shoulders.

She collapsed under him. His penis slipped out. She turned and lay on her back. Spreading her legs wide, she slapped him across the face, her lips drawn back in a snarl. "I want to feel more pain." Her voice came out in a growl. "Are you male enough to give it to me?"

"More than you think, bitch," he growled and shoved his rampant penis into her. She howled, wrapped her long legs around his torso and pulled him close, pressing her breasts against his heaving chest. Then she bit him on the shoulder. It hurt but he knew she had not pierced his skin.

She hammered her agile body into his, pumping her buttocks up and down, rippling her hot sheath the length of his hard penis. He came inside her milking pussy with a triumphant shout. Then he pulled out and stood swaying above her. She glared up.

"I'm not satisfied," she said, her voice cold.

He took the whip away from the Frog male and laid the leash across her flat, golden belly.

She cried out in surprise and stared at the red welts the leash had left on her smooth skin. She rose with fluid movements and stood, her legs planted apart, her chest falling and rising. "You dare to use the whip on the Golden Goddess?"

He whipped the tip across her breasts. "Isn't that what you want, bitch?" he growled, almost angry now.

Rushing him, she stared into his face with her large black eyes and then punched him in the belly. As the air whooshed out of him, he reached and clamped his hand around one of her arms. "You want to play rough? I can play the same way."

Wrapping her arms around his chest, she fell backward and pulled him down with her. They rolled on the floor like two wrestlers. His head felt heavy and for some reason he couldn't form any clear thoughts. He was an animal in heat and he needed to satisfy his lust. Angry, he pinned her to the floor, pried open her thighs and fell between them. Pushing his hard penis back into her, he fucked her with powerful strokes until she cried out and locked her strong legs behind his buttocks. He felt the pulsating walls of her vagina sucking and vibrating around his shaft.

Her discharge was hot and she screamed when she experienced another orgasm. He gave in to his own demands and filled her with his own hot spermatic fluid. Following a strong hunger inside him, he sank his teeth into her shoulder, felt blood entering his mouth, and swallowed. It tasted salty and warm. When the wave of insanity subsided and he regained his clear thinking, he stopped licking the wound in her shoulder.

They lay panting on the floor, wrapped in each other.

He felt tired and spent. His back and chest hurt from the lashes he had received. She released him and watched with lazy eyes as he rose looking down over her. A small trickle of blood painted a red streak down her golden shoulder onto the unblemished skin of her breast.

She smiled and lifted an arm to let him pull her up.

"Pain and pleasure," she said softly as she molded her warm body against his. "They are one and the same. One cannot exist without the other." She laughed. "You have performed well, Earthman. Now, go and pleasure a few of the young females. They are waiting for you."

He looked down at his limp member. "I'm afraid I may have a problem there."

She shrugged. "That is not a problem. The leaves from the *Flowers of Fertility* will solve your dilemma." She nodded to one of the girls, who came close and offered Stark a handful of the red petals.

"Go on. Chew on them. They will lend you strength and endurance."

With some apprehension, he let the girl put some of the petals into his mouth. She watched him as he carefully chewed. T'Phira had been correct. It didn't take long until his penis strutted proudly between his legs and the desire in him was strong to put it into the tight pussy of the girl who gave him the petals.

As if reading his thoughts, the girl took his hand and pulled him with her. She knelt on the floor and waited for him to mount her. Her sheath was soft and tight, but he managed to slide easily into its greased hot inferno. While he pumped into the young female's taut buttocks, he saw a number of the other young Frog girls coming closer. They were touching each other's pussies to satisfy some of their desire, but he knew that he was the one they ultimately wanted.

They lined up beside the girl he was fucking. On their knees and their buttocks lifted up, they waited for him to put his weapon into their creamy sheaths.

When the girl in front of him finished panting and bucking, he moved over the next girl and entered her eager pussy. Someone offered him something to drink. He swallowed the liquid without thinking. It lent him strength and, with renewed vigor, he kept pounding into the hot pussy between the young female's clenching buttocks.

How many Frog girls he fucked, he didn't know. He found himself lying on T'Phira's bed, exhausted and hurting.

Pain and pleasure. They are not the same. They are as opposite as night and day, good and evil, but you are right, Golden Goddess. One cannot exist without the other.

Chapter Seven

Borton plucked the strings of his musical instrument with great skill and his baritone voice rang through the morning air.

Stark leaned on his spear and listened, enjoying the other man's voice and words.

High above the eagle flies
Over the mountains in the blue skies
On powerful wings the giant bird glides
While through the forest the wanderer strides
He sees the eagle high above
And mourns his long lost love
Slavers took her away in one of their ships
Never again will he taste her ruby red lips
Across his back he carries a sword
In his mind...

He stopped singing when a group of Frogs came into view. "I believe you'll be leaving me again for the day," he said to Stark.

Stark watched the group coming closer. Borton had been correct. They indicated with gestures that he should come with them. He had no doubt where he would be going again.

On silent wings a spaceships soars
To carry his love away...

Borton's voice faded in the distance as Stark entered the narrow jungle path that led to T'Phira's palace.

She stood at one of the windows and looked outside. When she heard Stark walking across the floor, she turned.

Brushing her golden hair out of her face, she gave him a friendly smile. "I want you to go swimming with me today," she said.

"Okay."

"But first we must get rid off that hair covering your face." She clapped her hands and one of the Frog girls came running, carrying a bowl filled with water and another bowl containing some kind of murky paste.

He knew he was going to get a shave, but looked forward to it with some apprehension.

"Lie down," T'Phira instructed him.

The Frog girl washed his beard with warm water. Then she proceeded to smear the murky paste into his beard. His face tingled as the paste hardened and he wondered how the girl would go about removing the hard shell that encased his face.

After a short time the girl began to peel off the crust. He felt a slight pinching and pulling but no real discomfort. The girl washed his face again and dried it with a silky cloth. Then she got up and left.

Stark ran his hand across his face and was pleased to find his skin soft and smooth.

He smiled happily. "I feel much better now," he said.

"I am glad," T'Phira said, smiling. "Now, come."

They walked down one of the paths that led to the lake. He looked across the calm water, wondering why she had chosen him to go swimming with her. The water was clear and he could see small creatures darting about close to the sandy bottom.

"Are you afraid of the water?" she asked, stretching her golden body. Her breasts gleamed in the light of the bright sun. She turned to present her shapely buttocks to his view. Throwing glances at him from under her long lashes, she teased him with her body, knowing how he would react.

He tried to control his longing for her, but was only partially successful.

She laughed when she saw his semi-erect penis and came close to him. Curling her long fingers around his penis, she stroked him with her warm hand. Then she pressed her breasts against his chest and grabbed his hard member with her thighs, jerking her hips back and forth. He could feel her moist labia caressing his penis.

"You want me?" she whispered, her black eyes staring into his.

"You know I do," he said hoarsely, putting his hands on her buttocks.

She twisted from his embrace and laughed, leaving him wanting.

"You are a bitch," he cursed under his breath.

"Go, cool off in the water," she said. Without looking back, she dove into the lake, cutting the water smoothly and leaving hardly a ripple.

He watched her disappear and put his foot into the warm, pleasant water. With a sigh, he jumped in and ducked his head under to cool down.

T'Phira was nowhere to be seen. He had seen the tiny slits under her arms and suspected she could breathe under water. As he stood waiting, she erupted out of the water not far from him, laughing, and spraying water.

"That feels good." She spread her arms and reached into the sky. "Here is where I am alive. In the water." She swam toward him with powerful strokes and came up in front of him. Grabbing his head, she planted a kiss on his lips. Letting go of him, she twisted around and presented her back. Pushing up her golden buttocks, she ordered, "Now you can put your organ into me."

He put his hands around her body and dug his fingers into her breasts, pulling her against him. Pressing his limp penis between her round buttocks, he hissed, "You are playing with me. You know damn well that I can't perform on command."

She rubbed her buttocks into his groin and managed to capture his member between them. He groaned as he felt his penis swelling in their soft grip. Pulling back, he forced it between her buttocks, found her anus and pushed. She struggled in his grip, but he held her and forced his hard pole into her, angry at the way she played with him.

Normally, he didn't care for anal intercourse, however this was not about sex but about domination, and he planned to dominate her this time. She was extremely tight and he almost gave up, but then he suddenly slid into her. She stopped struggling and let him fuck her his way. After a while, she moaned and rubbed against him. He grabbed a handful of her long hair and pulled back her head with one hand, with the other he held her by the throat.

"You like this?" he panted into her ear, thrusting back and forth. "You like this, bitch?"

Her hands reached behind her and with her fingers, she raked his pounding hips. "When you're finished I will show you what I like." She taunted him by rotating her buttocks and milking him.

He couldn't control his lust and exploded inside her tight channel, shouting loudly. He freed her from his embrace and she pulled forward. She turned and stood in front of him, her long, split tongue playing between her open lips like a living thing. Looking down, she stared at his penis as it stood proudly below his belly.

Before he could react, she threw her arms around his body and pulled him under the surface. Swimming into the deeper water, she held him with unexpected force. He tried to break her embrace but she kept his arms pinned to his sides.

His lungs threatened to burst when she let go. He shot upward, broke the surface, gulping for air. He could see her golden body in the water. Then he felt her tongue licking his belly. Her mouth moved down and closed over his penis, while her fingers dug into his buttocks.

Before she released him again, she bit down and sank her teeth into his member, hard enough for him to feel pain. Then she rose in front of him and wrapped her legs around his torso. Snapping her hips forward, she slipped her sheath over his penis.

"This is the way *I* like it," she said after spewing water into his face. Again, she pulled him with her under water. But this time she only submerged her own body.

He floated on top of her, holding her moving buttocks in his hands to make certain he didn't slip out of her as she fucked him from below. Her face was close to the surface and her black eyes stared up at him. She had her mouth open as she breathed in the water.

He realized she could easily drown him if she chose to do so. The water was her element and playground. He was only an intruder.

She must have sensed when he was ready to come. At the same moment he stiffened to shoot his load into her, she wrapped her strong legs around his quivering torso and pulled him under the surface. Taking him deep down, she didn't let go of him.

The threat and fear of drowning increased his orgasm to a height and length he had never achieved before. His lungs screamed for air, his body demanded more oxygen to ease the strain he put on his muscles as he pumped between T'Phira's clutching thighs. As his sperm shot into her and blackness descended upon him, his last thoughts were *please let me finish this unbelievable orgasm.*

But he didn't loose consciousness. Before he fully blacked out, T'Phira opened her thighs and dragged him with her to the surface. Sputtering water, his heart pounding in his chest, he gasped for air, letting her support him because his muscles were too weak to move his arms and legs.

"Did you enjoy that?" she asked, smiling cruelly.

"Best fuck I ever had," he said, still struggling for breath. Feeling the strength slowly creeping back into his limbs, he fought to stay above water. Angry at her for putting him through this, he put his hand between her legs and squeezed. "You want to do it again?" he asked.

She didn't smile when she looked at him. "If you insist, but let me warn you. This time it will kill you."

"Maybe, but this time I will be on guard," he said.

She reached for his penis and laughed. "This limp thing won't be any good to me. Come and swim with me. I want to show you my favorite place." She swam away but stopped and looked back when he didn't follow. "I won't let you drown, I promise," she called.

He swam after her, his limbs aching and his heart still beating fast. She slowed to let him catch up. He marveled at the way her supple body easily cut through the water. She was right, this was her element. Even though he was a good swimmer, in comparison he was awkward and slow. After a while she would dive under and swim around him, like a playful dolphin on Earth, but she didn't make any more attempts to pull him under the surface.

They were heading for the small island in the middle of the lake. T'Phira was the first one to reach it, which did not surprise Stark. He was still tired from his near fatal sexual encounter with her and had not been able to keep up with her.

He climbed onto land, wondering if he would have enough strength to return to the mainland.

T'Phira stood in the white sand and watched him as he knelt to catch his breath. He heard her soft, tinkling laughter. "I hope you recover fast, because I have plans for us," she said.

He looked up and squinted against the sun behind her back. It outlined her body in a way that made her appear like a golden vision. She stood with spread legs and her arms stretched away from her side. Like an angel.

He chuckled. *More like a seductive demon ready to suck the life-force out of me.*

Rising to his feet, he looked into her black eyes. He was not going to show any weakness. "I'm ready for whatever you have planned for me. In fact, I'm looking forward to it."

"Good. Now, come with me into my little retrieve where we will be undisturbed. Sometimes I need to get away from everyone and just be by myself, especially when I feel homesick. Today is one of those days, but I will share this day with you."

A narrow path wound its way through the thick vegetation and Stark inhaled the moisture-laden air of this little piece of jungle. He became aware of chirping insects and flying animals and wondered if any large predators might hide in the protection of the undergrowth or even in the canopy that shaded the ground from the sun.

The path ended abruptly and Stark stood silent for a moment to take in the peaceful scene he saw.

T'Phira watched him and smiled. "Welcome to my little piece of Paradise," she said.

"This is beautiful." Stark took a few steps toward the pond and looked into the crystal clear water. He saw small creatures swimming close to the surface; creatures that looked like long pencils with heads too large for their bodies. They stuck out their heads and stared up at him out of protruding eyes, their skinny legs treading water to keep them from sinking under the surface.

Laughing, T'Phira bent down and put her hand into the water. The little creatures swam around her hand and touched it with their tiny snouts. "These are my friends," she said. "Go and pick some of the red seed from the trees. They like those seeds but they can't get to them. They are prisoners of the water, unlike me."

Stark searched for the trees and found them growing everywhere. They were laden with clusters of tiny fruit. He picked a handful and threw them into the water. The little creatures gobbled them up from the surface where they floated like tiny red bubbles.

When Stark put his hand into the water, he was greeted by a swarm of nibbling mouths. Reflex made him pull back his hand, but T'Phira laughed. "They can't bite you. They have no teeth."

"What are they?"

She shrugged. "Just creatures of the water. Creatures without malice, who don't judge you and who demand nothing from you."

He threw her an inquiring look. "Who judges you? You are the queen of your people."

"Yes, I am a queen, worshipped as a goddess even, but my subjects are not my people. You may have noticed that I do not look like them."

"Of course I have, but I thought you were possibly a mutation."

"Well, you thought wrong. I am not a mutation. There are others like me. My mother was taken from her people when she was young and kept prisoner by the *Wild Ones*. I am her daughter. My father is one of the males who raped her over and over. When I was old enough to suffer the same fate, I escaped and found refuge with the *Wkyt'sij* who made me their queen and goddess. I love them, but I am not one of them." She rose and gazed across the small glade. "This is where I seek solitude and dream about one day returning to my people."

Stark studied her, as she stood almost forlorn beside the pond, her black eyes staring into nothingness. "I also was taken from my people," he said quietly. "And I also wish to return."

Her eyes focused on him. "Sometimes we have to accept our fate," she said. Then she smiled and opened her arms. "Let us not mourn what we have lost but embrace the present and what we have. Come to me."

He stepped into her embrace. She ran her fingers across his cheeks and gazed into his eyes. "I sense something about you that is different from Borton. A power deep inside you, a strength that is beyond even your own understanding. I sensed this the first time you lay in my arms, the first time you entered my body and let down your guard. What am I sensing?"

Stark shrugged. "I'm not sure what you are talking about. I am just an ordinary man, nobody special. And right now I am extremely horny."

She laughed. "Go and eat some of those red seeds. They will give you stamina and increase the pleasure you will experience when we copulate."

Not quite certain if he should ingest something that might prove fatal to his system, he nevertheless picked some of the seeds and put them into his mouth. They tasted a bit tardy but not unpleasant. He picked more and carried them to T'Phira, offering them to her. She licked them out of his hand and smiled wickedly.

Stepping back, she watched him with lazy eyes. Something was happening to him as he stood looking at her. He felt lightheaded and his penis seemed to be on fire. It burned with blistering heat and when he put his hand on it, it felt like touching a hard piece of wood.

His eyes played tricks on him. Instead of seeing T'Phira, he saw a baldheaded, glowing creature with burning eyes and unfurled wings. Her breasts were larger than he remembered and her mound was thick and red. She came closer and put a clawed hand on his chest.

"Lie down," she ordered with a gravelly sounding voice.

He sank to the soft ground and stretched out on his back. She stood over him with her legs spread and stared at him out of fiery eyes. Slowly, she bent her knees and lowered her body, her red-framed vagina hovering above the tip of his throbbing penis.

The thick labia parted as she sank onto his penis. Still hovering, she rubbed her velvety slit slowly across his penis. Her mouth opened and, with a loud hiss, her long forked tongue emerged between two needle thin canines and played across her lips.

The soft touch of her labia sent delicious shivers down his spine, and when she slipped her tight sheath over his straining penis, he let out a shout of joy as the sweet sensation flooded through his body.

Her spread wings moved like a black cape behind her, blocking out the burning sun, as she writhed on top of him, her bright eyes never leaving his face.

"Are you real or just a figment of my imagination?" he asked, fighting the urge to shoot his essence into her clutching vagina.

She laughed with a hollow sound. "You see what you want to see, Earthman," she said. "Just relax and enjoy the moment." Her image blurred and her upper body seemed to change. The beak of a bird grew out of her face and the shape of her eyes became round, framed by a circle of thick skin. Her breasts shrank to turn into small bumps with tiny nipples.

Her lower body stayed the same, except now it seemed to be covered with a fine carpet of soft feathers. She moved her whole body with sinuous grace above him, her vagina an envelope of hot flesh around his pole. He grabbed her grinding hips and pulled her into his lap, pushing up against her, shouting hoarsely as he emptied his load into her.

She let out a series of deep chirping noises and clamped down hard on his throbbing penis, her vagina walls sucking rhythmically. Her hot discharge ran down between his buttocks, signaling that she was experiencing her own orgasm.

When they were both finished, she lifted up and freed his still throbbing organ. Getting to her knees, she waited for him to kneel behind her and pushed up her rounded posterior. Her wings were gone and now he could see a short fin running from the base of her spine up to her head where it grew into a high sail. Tiny, silvery scales covered her whole body, and when he put his hands around her chest to feel for her breasts, they had grown again to their normal size.

He put his penis between her spread thighs and searched for her vagina. She moaned and lifted up when his hard flesh touched her fat lips, grabbing him like a soft vice. Feeling his penis entering her warm channel, he pushed forward and slid easily into her welcoming sex-organ.

Milking him softly, she rotated her buttocks while he knelt behind her, his hands on her hips. She moaned with a low, hissing sound, and after awhile she jerked her hips frantically, panting and crying out unintelligible sounds.

He stroked her silvery back with one hand. It felt smooth and satiny, like normal skin, not scaly and hard as one might expect. The fine scales covering her body were soft and pliable and warm. In fact, he could see tiny droplets of perspiration forming on her back from the continuous strain produced by her frantic movements.

She fell forward, making him slip out of her. With one fluid movement, she turned under him onto her back. Gasping, she clung to him and pulled him between her widespread silvery thighs. Clutching his hips with her knees, she managed to sheath his stabbing penis and took him back into her.

"Show no mercy," she almost screamed. "I need to feel pain!" Her face was pulled into a savage, ferocious mask, but he found it beautiful in its alien wildness.

He felt like a primeval beast and fucked her with brutal strokes. She raked his back with long fingernails, and he knew that she was drawing blood. He didn't feel any pain, only pleasure beyond anything he ever experienced before.

His rational mind, whatever was left of it, wondered what was in those berries he had ingested. He was like a wild man, consumed by lust and possessed with an endurance that allowed him to go on forever.

T'Phira displayed strength and ferocity matching his as she bucked underneath him, her lower body slamming against his with relentlessness.

He climaxed numerous times without losing fluid, and T'Phira seemed to experience one continuous orgasm.

"It is time," she cried out, clamping her long legs around his torso. "Time for the final moment!"

He knew what she wanted and was ready. With a roar that echoed through the small glade, he crushed her slender body to him. His rampant penis jumped inside her clutching vagina and his sperm spewed into her with explosive force. His lips found her throat. Opening his mouth, he sank his teeth into the tender meat of her neck, drank from the blood that trickled from her punctured vein.

His mind expanded and touched the fabric of the universe for a nanosecond that lasted an eternity as he reached the apex of his climax.

He knew everything.

He knew and understood the universe, knew the beginning, knew the end. He was aware of every single life form and organism created by the very essence of the life force that was the universe.

He was the universe.

Then he floated in the empty, endless void.

Alone and searching.

Opening his eyes, he found he was lying on a carpet of soft grass. The sun had disappeared behind the canopy of treetops above him. He turned his head when he heard the splashing of water. Sitting up, he suddenly remembered where he was. Looking around, he didn't see T'Phira anywhere. He rose to his feet and walked toward the small pond and stared into the clear water, expecting to see the tiny creatures, but they were gone.

Feeling a dull pain all over his body, most of it concentrated on his back, he noticed the crusted blood on his arms and his upper torso. He grimaced as memory flooded back. Still feeling T'Phira's nails raking his back, he could only imagine what his back must look like.

"T'Phira?" he called.

As he searched the pond, he saw her golden body lying under the surface in the water, facedown without moving, her arms and legs spread away from her body. At first, he thought she was dead, drowned, but then he remembered that she could breathe under water.

When he looked closer, he could see her body covered by those tiny creatures. They darted back and forth, nibbling on her skin. While he watched, she turned onto her back, but she didn't see him because her eyes were closed.

He sat down in the grass and waited for her, enjoying the peace and silence of this little piece of paradise.

Darkness was fast descending as she rose from the water and climbed back on dry land. Her face looked serene. She stepped up to him and smiled, appearing happy and content. He searched for the wound his teeth must have left in her neck but only saw a couple of pink puncture marks.

He was disturbed by what had made him behave like a mad bloodthirsty creature of the night. The memory of what had transpired was unclear. He barely remembered the taste of her slightly salty blood, but remembering he did.

"Come, let's get back to the real world," she said softly, taking his hand. "You have given me what I craved."

Chapter Eight

When Stark saw the two broad-shouldered figures in their tight black outfits, he heaved a sigh of regret. Looking around, he knew there was no escape. The walls of the nearby jungle didn't provide a refuge and neither did the misty lake. He watched them come closer, accepting his fate.

The Melkos had found him.

Not saying anything, they only stared with their cold eyes.

Stark searched for Borton but the other man was not nearby, which was maybe a good thing. He didn't know if they had come only for him or if they had come for both of them. Maybe if they didn't see Borton, they may leave him alone.

He walked between them like a sheep led to be slaughtered. He didn't know what awaited him. Whatever it was, he would deal with it when it arrived. They boarded a small tear-shaped vehicle. It lifted into the air and headed away from the village of the Frog people.

Through the front window, he could see the palace of the Golden Goddess disappearing below them and wondered if she would miss him. He thought of Feleena. He hadn't seen her since their capture by the Frog people and he feared for her safety, but somehow he could no bring himself to believe that the Frogs would hurt her in any way. They had seemed savage at first, but he knew they did have compassion for other living beings.

T'Phira showed him a side of her that wasn't soft and cuddly. She loved to give and receive pain, but she had not been cruel enough to inflict serious injury on him. His body still itched from the welts the leash left and from her sharp nails when she raked them across his skin, but the pain was negligible and nearly gone.

He stared at the wide shoulders of the two Melkos in the seats in front of him, suppressing thoughts of escape. He was certain that this time he would not get a second chance. Maybe it was better to let them take him wherever it was he was supposed to be. His chances of escape might be better there. There was no refuge in the jungle, as he had found out.

He relaxed in his seat and even managed to sleep a little. When he awoke and looked out of the front window he saw what looked like a small city at the edge of an ocean. The airboat landed in front of a flat building. Stark's captors escorted him across the tarmac toward the building.

He watched a large group of people coming out of another building. They marched in double file, heading for a transporter parked nearby. The members of the group looked humanoid. All were dressed in skintight red outfits. A transparent helmet covered each head. Two armed Melkos walked behind them.

Stark wondered where they were headed and why they wore what looked like diving suits.

Inside the building, he was taken into the custody of a couple of guards, who took him into a large room filled with other prisoners.

* * * *

The naked feet of the woman tapped a monotonous rhythm on the cool plastic tabletop. Rotating her naked body, she laughed with a gurgling sound. Her four breasts jiggled as she moved her upper body. She shook back her long red hair and it cascaded down to her fleshy buttocks and wide hips.

Increasing the speed of her moving hips, she pumped her pubic area back and forth suggestively. Her orange skin shone wet in the artificial light emitting from the walls and ceiling.

The men sitting at the tables encouraged her with loud calls and clicking of tongues.

Stark watched her with little interest, lost in his thoughts. Without really hearing what they said, he listened to the conversation of a couple of men near him.

"You should have visited Elbos, my friend. The women there have six breasts. Three on each side."

"Really? Six breasts. Are they large? I like women with large breasts."

"So do I. It is hard to believe that there are many races where the women have only two breasts?"

"Yes, I know. I guess there is nothing wrong with that if they are large enough." The speaker looked at Stark. "Hey you...you seem to belong to one of those races."

The question ripped Stark out of his brooding thoughts. He stared at the speaker but didn't answer him.

"You've only just arrived," the other one said and studied Stark with veiled curiosity.

He scrutinized the two men in turn. It was evident that they belonged to the same race as the woman dancing on the table. Thick, red hair hung past their wide shoulders. Except for their orange skin color they could not be distinguished from a human man. It surprised him to see their clean-shaven faces. He ran his fingers through his beard.

"Do you understand us?" The speaker gave Stark a curious stare.

"Maybe his translator doesn't work properly," the second man said.

Stark smiled. "I understand you quite well," he said slowly. "I'm just taking my time to get used to all of this."

"What system are you from? I've only seen a few men with such skin color. Your skin is light but not as white as the Melkos," the second, the older of the two men, said. His brown eyes gazed at Stark with open interest.

"I am from Earth," Stark informed them.

"Earth?"

"Yes Earth, the third planet in the Solar system."

The man drew his brows together. "I've been to many systems and I know the most important ones toward the center of the Galaxy, but I've never heard of Earth. In which zone is Earth's system?"

Stark shrugged. "I don't know. Until recently, I only knew that Earth is the third planet circling a sun with nine other planets. The only planet populated by an intelligent race. My system is located at the edge of the Milky Way. That's what we call the Galaxy. I've never given much thought to other suns or other planets, not to mention alien life forms."

The other man shook his head. He looked at is companion. "Must be one of the unexplored barbaric systems at the edge." He turned back to Stark and clapped him on the shoulder. "Welcome to the rest of the Galaxy."

Stark grinned crookedly. "Great welcome. I'm a slave."

The older man nodded. "That you are. We are all slaves. It's not so bad, though. Behave yourself and make an effort in finding Krestoll and you won't mind it so much. There are places worse than this one." He laughed. "Come on. Let's join the others and take part in the Game. Maa-laci is the prize."

Maa-laci was the woman dancing on the table. She jumped onto the floor and walked over to the circle of men involved in some kind of game. Her movements were cat-like and sensuous.

"She's only just arrived, just like you. She grew up in one of our colonies. Our women are usually not this wild." He watched the woman walking across the floor and sighed. "I can't believe such fire in a *Katawoman*."

Stark had to agree. The displayed wildness of Maa-laci had left an impression on him, even though he had not paid too much attention to her. The sight of her four breasts had aroused his curiosity for a short time, but then he kept thinking about Feleena, wondering what might have happened to her.

He and his two new companions joined the other men in the circle and soon his mind was occupied with other thoughts.

The orange-skinned woman danced inside the circle of men. She moved her upper body and hips to the rhythm of their clapping hands and Stark had to admit there was something hypnotic in her movements. He watched her perspiring body undulate and noted her solid buttocks and breasts.

Barely aware of what he was doing, his hands reached for the cube-sticks and threw them onto the floor, his gaze glued to the whirling, dancing body of the woman in the circle.

Stopping abruptly and glaring at him, she approached and grabbed his hand.

"You are the winner," she said. Her voice sounded soft and alluring. "Come with me. I belong to you for one sleep period." Her hand touched his naked arm. "You look strong. I think I will enjoy you."

Her dark eyes seemed distant, unfocussed. She pressed her naked body against his. "Come," she whispered. "Let us not waste time."

"Not so fast," growled a deep voice behind Stark.

He turned to look into the bearded face of the speaker. He was big, mean-looking and at least a head taller than Stark, who stood six foot two.

"What is the problem?" he asked.

The small yellow eyes of the giant sparkled evilly. Growling, he pulled his thick upper lip to expose a pair of long canines. "What is the problem? Do you need to ask? Maa-laci belongs to me. Do you know who I am?"

"I'm new here, which means I don't know anybody, not even you, whoever you might be," Stark said cautiously.

The giant grabbed Stark's throat with one large hand. "I am Corbo. From now on if you want something you ask me first, understood?"

"Why?" Stark struggled to dislodge the big man's hand.

"Because I am Corbo!"

"I know that, but you are a slave...like me," Stark said defiantly.

The giant hand squeezed Stark's throat. "Don't question me again, ever! I am the strongest and the biggest here. If I want you dead, you die. Everything that happens here goes through me," he roared. Then he threw Stark against the nearest wall, where he lay dazed.

Looking up, he saw the bulky figure of Corbo bending over him.

What's wrong with me? I can't seem to formulate any clear thoughts.

He lifted his hands trying to defend himself. The giant laughed and kicked him in the ribs.

Something exploded inside Stark. Strength flooded through his stunned body and, without effort, he pulled the strong fingers of the giant from his throat. Rising, he grabbed the big man, lifted him above his head and heaved him across the room. Like a shadow, he followed and brought his fist down hard in the fat neck of his opponent.

The giant collapsed without a sound. Stark stared at the big man's exposed throat, fighting the urge to sink his teeth into its soft flesh.

Stark turned away and looked at the silent, watching crowd. A deep growl filled the air and he realized it came from his own throat as his lips curled in a snarl. Onlookers stepped back when they looked into his face and exclaimed loudly.

Some of the bystanders whispered, "His eyes...", but he didn't know what they meant.

Maa-laci rushed him and stroked his chest. "You are strong," she whispered. "What's your name?"

"I'm David," he said, shaking off her hands. "Leave me alone. I have to think."

She frowned and stepped in front of him. "I'll make you forget whatever it is that bothers you. I can do things with my body not many females can do. You won't regret it." She pulled on his hand. "Don't deny me."

"You are right," he said, looking at her four breasts. A sudden desire for this alien woman rose inside him. "Maybe you can make me forget that I'm a prisoner on a strange planet, possessed by something I can't explain. Something that creates a hunger in me that can't seem to be stilled. Maybe I'll wake up and discover this is only a crazy dream."

Maa-laci pulled him to her sleeping quarters. When she saw him looking at the six empty cots, she chuckled happily. "All the others are busy entertaining some male. We will be alone for most of the night. Take off your clothing and let me get a better look at my master for tonight."

She helped him remove his shirt and pants. As he stood naked, her eyes widened and, running her hands across his deep chest, she purred, "You are quite a handsome specimen of a male." His erect penis touched her belly. She laughed and took it into her hand. "I hope his performance matches his appearance," then licked her lips with a moist tongue.

Kneeling on the floor, her upper body resting on her cot, she pushed up her fleshy buttocks. "I like to start with an easy position," she said over her orange shoulder.

He dropped down behind her and put his finger into the crease between her buttocks. Stroking her puckered anus, he moved his finger lower and caressed her slit. She moaned and pushed back, letting him slide his finger into her moist canal. He pushed back and forth, finger-fucking her with slow movements.

She moaned loudly and squeezed her vagina walls around his finger. "I need something bigger," she cried out.

He pulled out his finger and put his hard penis between her orange cheeks, teasing her enflamed sex-organ by rubbing the head of his penis over her clitoris.

"Now," she called out. "Fuck me now!"

He took hold of her wide hips and pushed forward, sliding deep into her hot sheath. She began bucking immediately, milking his penis with ferocious movement. He held her between his strong hands, slowing the rotation of her buttocks. She came with a loud piercing cry, squeezing the length of his penis and digging her hands into the blanket covering her cot.

He hammered into her for a long time but didn't climax.

"Let's change positions," she cried suddenly. "My knees are getting sore."

He let her stretch out on the cot. Spreading her thighs wide, she pulled her legs up until her knees touched her shoulders. He moved on top of her and entered her again. Her four breasts felt strange on his chest and it turned him on immensely.

Forgetting about the fight with Corbo and his worries about Feleena's well-being, he fucked her with deep thrusts, enjoying her yielding body. She proved to be extremely flexible and used her ability to bend her body into nearly impossible positions that made their sexual encounter exceedingly pleasurable.

When he sensed the presence of someone in the room, he turned his head to see who it was. In the semidarkness, he saw one of the females who shared the room with Maa-laci crawl onto her cot. Even though she appeared to be uninterested, Stark knew that she was quite aware of them. It was difficult, to ignore Maa-laci's loud moans and the noise of the squeaking cot as Stark pounded between her clutching thighs.

His need for relief from his desire to experience his final orgasms inside the alien woman's hot vagina had reached the point of being uncontrollable and he let go. As he exploded inside the clasping walls of her sheath, he ignored the presence of the other woman and shouted hoarsely as the pleasure roared through his body.

When he was finished, he collapsed and lay on top of Maa-laci's heaving body, supported by her soft four breasts.

Only faintly, he heard the other woman say, "I wish my partner would have had the stamina and skill you possess, Beastman. Only a savage beast can fulfill Maa-laci's desires and you seem to have given her what she craves. I've never seen her on her back after her encounters. If you have some energy left, maybe you can join me on my cot and give me some of that passion."

Maa-laci chuckled under Stark. "Tarma is right. You are an exceptional specimen. Maybe you should accept her invitation. I am too tired to move."

Stark disengaged his body from her embrace and sat up. He smiled at Tarma. "Any other time I might accept but Maa-laci has sucked me dry. Perhaps another time."

"Too bad." Tarma sighed.

He could see her sitting on her cot, her upper body exposed. She was slim, her breasts were small, but she had only two. Her face was hidden in the shadows and he didn't know what she looked like. Maybe it was just as well. Just because she had a humanoid body didn't mean her face was human-like.

He dressed and, after touching Maa-laci on her shoulder, he walked past the woman on the other cot. He thought he saw the glint of what looked like a beak on her face, but that could have been an illusion.

Closing the door behind him, he walked back to his own quarters.

Chapter Nine

Stark studied the other nine prisoners in his group. Four of them were female. Their slim bodies were sharply displayed in their skintight suits. One of them had four breasts. At first, he assumed it was Maa-laci, but then he saw her face and realized she didn't even belong to Maa-laci's race. The second woman looked human, except for her four arms.

When his gaze wandered to the third one, he noticed that the form of her body wasn't any different from that of a human woman. Her face, though, was totally alien. Instead of a mouth and nose she had a yellow beak. In her strangeness she emitted a magical attraction and he found her exotic and exciting. She noticed his eyes on her and opened her beak. He heard the twittering of a bird, but his translator made her words understandable.

"I've never seen you before. You must be new."

He nodded. "Yes, I am. They call me David."

"And I am Girri," she said. "You've mined Krestoll before?"

"No, I don't have any idea what I'm facing."

"Don't worry. We'll teach you. It is not so bad."

Stark smiled. "Thank you." He was bewitched by her melodic voice. Turning his attention to the men, he saw that one of them was the giant Corbo.

The big man had not bothered Stark after their short fight. He had just simply ignored him. Stark had misgivings about the giant's presence.

A slight vibration ran through the ship.

"We have arrived," said the man beside Stark. He reached up and released the helmet that hung above his head.

Stark followed his example and fastened the helmet to the ring on his suit. It sealed itself with a barely audible click. He took a few experimental breaths and found he could breathe. He didn't quite understand the principle how he could breathe at all without an oxygen tank strapped to his back, but one of the men had explained it to him briefly when he asked him about the diving suits they wore.

"They are airtight and pressure resistant. The helmets are equipped with an oxygen extractor. As the word says, they extract oxygen from the air and the water. I can't go into details because I don't know how they work."

Stark had been skeptic; still was.

The submarine was far below the surface and he had misgivings about what the pressure would do to his system, and when he swam out of the airlock, he experienced a moment of claustrophobia. It only lasted a short time, and he realized that he felt no discomfort.

The others had been swimming away from the ship and he followed them, trying to catch up. The flippers on his feet propelled him forward, but when he tried to use his arms, he became aware of the object in his hands. He remembered someone handing it to him before he left the ship. He had paid little attention, his mind occupied with the possible danger he might have to face.

One of the swimmers ahead of him stopped and waited for him. "Come on, hurry up. It is dangerous to swim alone."

He recognized Girri's twittering voice.

Stark reached her. She noticed the object in his hands. "I see they gave you a *Destructor*. why you're so slow. Click it onto the magnetic strip on the side of your right leg and free your arms."

Stark followed her advice, cursing silently.

I wish they'd given me some instructions.

After that, he and Girri caught up with the others in a short time, and Stark was happy to have at least on friend who seemed to care about his safety.

A dark shadow floated That's above them and he noticed that the group pulled closer together.

"It seems we have Parsas for company," Corbo's voice announced.

"Parsas?" Stark asked. "What are Parsas?"

"Dangerous predators," Girri explained.

Corbo's mocking laughter sounded loud in Stark's helmet. "Don't be too eager to meet them, wild man. I have a feeling we'll be seeing more of them before this work period is over. I hope you are as good with a *Destructor* as you are with your fists."

As if to underline his words, two huge, dark shadows drifted by on either side of them. Silently and without creating too much commotion, the group of divers swam toward its destination, staying close together.

"How far is it still?" Stark asked in a whisper.

"We should be there soon," answered a female voice. He didn't know which of them had spoken, but he was grateful that the group seemed to have accepted him. "Thank you," he said, "whoever you are."

The diver beside him touched his helmet with a fleeting gesture. "You are welcome."

He glanced at the swimming figure, realized it was the female with the four arms. She glided through the water with apparent ease, using two of her arms for swimming and the other two to carry a weapon identical to the one Stark had clipped to his side.

"I'm Xloni," she said.

"I am David."

She laughed softly. "I know. We all know. There are no secrets when we are wearing these helmets."

In the light from the torches on everyone's helmet, he saw a dark wall appearing in front of them. The group stopped swimming and he discovered solid rock under his feet.

"We have arrived," Girri's voice told him. She swam up to him and touched his arm. "Be on guard," she said. "Our lives may be in Xloni's and your hands."

"You stay here," Xloni told him. "I'll take the watch further down."

He watched everyone swimming away as they headed for a shimmering surface in the rock wall. As he watched, he saw some of them removing tools from their backpacks. They began cutting chunks of rock out of the shimmering wall with brightly burning lasers beams, while the others put the chunks into large nets.

He noticed that the ones who were cutting into the rock wall didn't do so randomly. One of the men searched the wall with some kind of instrument before any of the others started cutting.

Looking around, Stark saw that the rock he floated on ended a few feet away. The light of his torch didn't penetrate far into the dark water below him, and he realized that he was looking into a deep chasm. Staring into the deep unknown, he felt alone and insignificant and gripped his weapon with fingers threatening to loose their strength.

While contemplating his fate, a large, dark shadow shot suddenly out of the depth, heading straight for him. A huge maw filled with ripping teeth gaped in front of him and, without thinking, he lifted his weapon and pushed the firing stud.

Bright fire exploded; the recoil from the released energy pushed him back. Tumbling in the water, he saw the huge creature floating by; the displaced water dragged him along and smashed him against the rocks.

"Are you all right?"

He heard the voice coming from far away and clung to it.

"David! Are you all right?" the voice asked again. Recognizing Xloni's voice, he attempted to regain his balance.

A face hovered in front of his. A deep ridge of bone shaded a pair of dark eyes. He didn't know who he looked at, but he could guess. "Xloni?" he asked.

She chuckled, exposing two thin fangs. "The one and only. Congratulations. Your first encounter with a *Parsa* and you survived. Good shooting."

"You mean I got it?"

"Not much left of the head."

"Everything happened so fast," Stark said.

"That's the way these things usually happen. They don't give you any warning. Come and have a look at your trophy."

She swam away. He followed, still a bit shaken up from the encounter.

As Xloni had said, there wasn't much left of the head, but the body of the Parsa floated lifeless in the water. It seemed to be some kind of giant serpent.

"Another of these beasts gone," Corbo's voice growled inside Stark's helmet. He gave him a thud between the ribs. "You are all right, wild man."

Stark found it ironic that the bearded giant would call him *wild man*. If anyone deserved to be called that it would be Corbo.

"Watch out!" Another man's voice warned sharply.

Stark swung around, his weapon up. But this time Xloni reacted before he did. Her weapon discharged but she missed. The long sinuous giant body shot by them.

"We'd better get back to the ship," Corbo said. "This carcass will attract all the predators in the neighborhood. We have enough Krestoll to fill our quota for the day."

Nobody argued and soon the group was on its way back to the safety of the ship. When they entered the airlock, Stark breathed a sigh of relief. Wary and tired, he sank onto his seat and closed his eyes. His first day collecting Krestoll had apparently gone well. He wasn't looking forward to the rest of his captivity.

A slap on his shoulder made him open his eyes. "Get out. You can sleep tonight in your quarters!"

He gave the Melkos an angry glare and cursed silently. Then he followed the others out of the ship.

When he arrived in the changing room, he found that another group of Krestoll miners had returned at the same time his own group did. He held his breath and nearly shouted with joy when he saw the naked back of one of the females. Her black hair spilled down across her shoulders.

He approached her and put his arms around her from behind. "Feleena," he cried out.

She turned around in his arms and stared at him with wide cat's eyes. He let go of her and stepped back. "I'm sorry. I thought you were someone else."

The female gave him a mocking smile. "Seems to me you can't wait until sleep period. You males are always horny." She moved her hips suggestively. "But if you insist, we can couple right here."

He smiled back, amazed at the similarity between this woman and Feleena. The same blue cat's eyes, the same petite figure and the same finely chiseled beautiful face. "Thank you for the offer, but what I said is the truth. You really do look a lot like someone I know. In fact, you two could almost be sisters."

"What is her name?"

"Feleena," he said.

She shook her head. "I don't know anyone by that name. By the way, I am Serina." She came closer and pressed her naked body against his. "Where is this Feleena?"

He shrugged, inhaling her slightly musky smell. "I don't know. I'm not even sure if she is here in this compound."

Her breasts touched his chest. Her cat's eyes studied him. "If she is not here and you long for her company, maybe I can take her place. You look like a capable male." She laughed softly. "I'm heading for the showers. Perhaps you want to join me there."

She slipped away on light feet. He watched her, his loins and heart pounding, feeling a strange attraction toward her. The same attraction he had felt toward Feleena.

Hearing someone approaching, he turned and looked at the four-armed woman coming toward him. He recognized Xloni's face.

She smiled. Her thin fangs gleamed white as she came closer. "So you are that new male who calls himself David." She touched his cheeks and looked into his eyes. Then she stepped back, shaking her long, blond hair out of her eyes. "I wondered what you looked like in the flesh."

"Do I pass inspection?" he asked, chuckling.

When she saw him staring at her ample breasts, she folded her four arms across them. "You seem to exude a strong magnetism." She studied him curiously. "I've never seen you before but I feel attracted to you. I find that strange because you're not even a member of my race."

"Maybe it's my charming personality." He laughed, surprised how easily he was accepting the fact that he was surrounded by so many different looking males and females. Even though Xloni didn't look like a human woman, he did experience a sexual attraction to her alien body.

Her legs were long, muscular, and well formed; her four arms smooth and not excessively muscular. The sight of them didn't repel him. Her breasts were large but solid. A thick carpet of hair covered her lower belly, hiding her genital area.

With a woman's intuition, she seemed to know what he was thinking. Smiling, she moved closer and pressed her naked breasts into his chest. Touching his semi-erect penis, she said, "If you're curious how it feels to enter my body, I will let you find out tonight. Come to my sleeping quarters. I am in section four."

He nodded. "I'm looking forward to it."

* * * *

She waited for him by the door to the room she shared with three other women. "I wasn't sure if you'd come," she said, greeting him with a kiss. "Come in. We are not alone but don't let that discourage you."

She pulled him into the room. All of the other five bunks were occupied. The females threw him curious glances but they didn't seem surprised at seeing him.

Xloni slipped out of her coveralls and watched him do the same. Naked, she lay on top of her cot and opened her legs. He stared at the rich carpet of hair. Actually, he preferred it when a woman shaved off her pubic hair. It looked more aesthetic and cleaner in his eyes, but that was just his preference. That didn't mean a woman with pubic hair didn't turn him on.

"Don't just look at it," she laughed. "It won't bite. I don't have teeth down there."

He grinned. "You are an alien woman to me. I don't know what to expect."

"I could say the same thing. How do I know that you won't use that appendix of yours to suck the blood from my veins?" She pumped her pelvis with suggestive motions. "Don't make me beg. Climb on top of me." Her eyes widened for a quick moment. "Or do you prefer it if I knelt on the floor. Some species only couple in that position. Or perhaps I should be on top?"

Laughing, he moved between her spread thighs and lay on top of her. "Any position is all right with me," he said.

Her hand reached between them and grabbed his penis. She gave a delighted little laugh. "You are quite hard. I wasn't even sure about that when you didn't react immediately to my invitation."

"Sometimes it is nice to be coaxed." He groaned as she stroked him gently. "Like that," he moaned. "You have a soft touch."

She pushed up against him. He felt soft, thick muscles grab the tip of his penis. Feeling a warm, slippery sheath enveloping the head of his organ, he thrust forward and slipped with ease into her. The soft walls of her vagina immediately began to ripple the length of his mast, and he knew he was going to have a satisfying experience.

It felt strange to have four arms around his back. Two of them moved down to his buttocks and grabbed them. The other two kept him in a tight embrace as he moved vigorously between her clutching thighs.

He didn't wait too long to have his first climax. When he came inside her hot canal, she moaned like a wounded animal and wrapped her legs around his thighs to keep him from pulling out when he was finished, but he had no such intentions.

"You are amazing." She whimpered loudly. "Most males are useless after their eruption."

"Usually I would be too," he said, "but somehow lately I've been able to have multiple orgasms. It must be the females I copulate with."

"Whatever the reason, I'm not complaining." She cried out as another orgasm racked her body. Hammering her hips, she doused his member with her hot discharge. "I believe I'm drying up," she moaned. "This has never happened to me before."

He didn't reply, just kept moving between her strong thighs, concentrating on the woman in his arms and trying to ignore the remarks from the other females watching.

Becoming aware of another pair of soft hands stroking his back, he turned his head to look at the female who stood beside the cot. "Care to change partners?" she asked. "It seems you fucked Xloni into exhaustion. That is something new."

Xloni released him from her embrace. Her arms and legs flopped onto the cot. "It is true, I am exhausted, but I'm not complaining. I feel totally satisfied."

He pulled out of her and eyed the other woman. She was tall and thin. He noticed that she had only two breasts and two arms. She was bald with a high forehead and her eyes glowed yellow in her narrow, elongated head. "My cot is over there." She pointed. Taking hold of his arm, she pulled him toward her cot.

"Lie down," she instructed. "I like to be on top."

He obliged her and watched her hovering above his strutting penis. "Watching and listening to you two didn't help my longing for a male," she said. "I hope you can last because my appetite is strong."

She sank into his lap and took him deeply into her with one swift motion. Then she moved up and down on his stiff pole, whipping her lower body with great speed and agility.

He watched her breasts bobbing on her thin body and noticed the extremely long nipples. Her vagina was bare of pubic hair and her labia almost nonexistent. But her sheath was hot and tight.

Fighting to last he managed to hold it for a long time and when he finally climaxed it came with a satisfying rush and tremendous power.

The alien woman let out a series of soft cries as she milked his discharge and experienced her own orgasm.

She collapsed on top of him when he was done but she didn't leave him and kept his member prisoner inside her throbbing vagina. "I need only a little," she whispered. He didn't quite understand what she meant.

"A little what?" he asked.

"Blood," she said softly.

When he expected her to sink her teeth into his neck, he was surprised when she just lay there, unmoving. Only her vagina seemed to be alive and he understood.

She was sucking blood from his penis.

He tried to push her off, but she made a hissing sound. "Please," she begged. "There is no danger to you. You won't miss it, but I need it badly." She put her lips on his and kissed him gently.

Her gentle kiss calmed him and her rhythmic squeezing of his penis made it swell inside her. Suddenly he felt extremely horny again and he grabbed her buttocks. She laughed softly into his mouth. Letting go of him, she said, "I have taken enough. If you want to put me onto my back and take control I will let you."

He nodded. "Let's do that."

She lifted up, and he watched his penis slide out. It didn't surprise him to see streaks of blood on it. She lay on her back and opened her legs wide. He entered her again and took his time to fuck her. There was no need to hurry. He wanted to enjoy it as long as she would let him. Somehow she had turned him on immensely.

She didn't lie immobile underneath him. Her thin body was as supple and agile as that of a snake and she writhed wildly under him, hissing passionately, making it hard for him to keep his slow movements steady. He held her churning narrow hips in his hands and thrust into her with powerful strokes. Where he found the strength he didn't care to know. As long as he could keep his organ hard inside her quaking vagina, he was happy.

He felt his orgasm approaching and knew it would be intense. He wasn't disappointed and suppressed his shouts of joy as he exploded inside her. He heard her ecstatic cries and closed her lips with his to keep her silent.

When he was done, she lay unmoving under him. Only her rasping breath gave him an indication that she was still conscious. His own breath was harsh in his ears, but he was satisfied.

Rising from the cot, he became aware of the other women in the room. They were sitting on their cots, watching him as he rose. Suddenly, he felt slightly embarrassed by his display of raw animal lust. He grimaced as they applauded.

"Perhaps tomorrow night you can spend some time in my bed," the nearest one said, thrusting out her four breasts.

"I believe I can entertain you all night. You are just the male who could awaken the deep passion I have inside me," another woman said.

He gave her a quick glance and wasn't sure if he'd want to awaken her passion. She was the only female in the room who barely resembled a human woman. Except for her breasts, her body was covered with long, yellow hair.

She smiled, displaying large teeth between thick, blue lips.

"Perhaps," he said politely. Giving the woman a crooked smile, he said, "I'd better get some rest now."

Chapter Ten

Deep in thought, Stark stared at the food cubes. Picking up one, he shoved it into his mouth without much enthusiasm. "Terrible stuff," he murmured. "I'd give anything for a descent piece of meat right now."

"Are you saying you eat parts of other living beings?" the man across from him exclaimed loudly.

Stark looked up and studied the man casually. Then he smiled. "Not parts of a living being. We kill it first. Besides, I don't eat raw meat."

"You surely must come from a barbaric race. No civilized being in the part of the Galaxy I come from would eat another." The man sounded upset and disgusted.

Stark gave him an amused smile. "On my planet there are many people who don't eat meat, only vegetables, but I don't believe they are any more civilized than I am. It's a matter of what you believe."

The other man made a face. "Savage," he murmured and lowered his eyes to concentrate on his food cubes.

Stark turned his head when the man beside him touched his arm.

"Don't hold it against him," the man said softly. "Borkuu comes from a planet whose inhabitants have reached a high level of enlightenment. There haven't been any wars among his race for millennia. There is no crime, therefore no need for punishment. He eats only synthetic foods, nothing grown naturally. His people are long-lived and the extinction of life, animal or plant, is a violation of his principles."

Stark shrugged. "I have no problem with that, as long as he doesn't try to force me to live by his ethics."

"Don't worry, he won't." The man smiled. "It is against his beliefs. He does not condone violence or force. By the way, I am called Akros and I share your craving for meat. I also come from a barbaric planet."

Stark studied the man and suppressed a shudder when he looked into his small yellow eyes.

That is not hard to believe. I hope he's not a cannibal.

Then he laughed. If he would have met this man on Earth a month ago, he would have been uneasy, to say the least, possibly doubted his sanity and wondered if he had met a young Sasquatch, but now he looked upon the ape-like being as just another slave.

The man rubbed a large paw across his hairy cheek and pulled his lips into a smile, exposing long canines. "Do you have a name?"

Stark nodded. "My name is David Stark. I come from a planet called Earth." He held out his hand.

Akros looked at the offered hand. Taking it into his large paw, he said, "I am familiar with this gesture. It proposes peace and removes the barrier that might exist between strangers when they meet."

"It might also have disastrous consequences," a voice growled behind Stark. "On my world reaching toward another man is a form of aggression."

Stark chuckled and moved over to make room for Corbo when the big man tried to squeeze his bulk into the seat beside him. Reaching for one of the food cubes on the tray in front of him, Corbo stuffed it between his teeth. "It's a crime that a man has to take food in this form," he growled.

Akros and Stark laughed. "We can't agree more," Stark said. "I've been wondering about something. Do the Melkos eat this kind of food?"

"Who knows what they eat, those white-faced demons," Corbo rumbled. "Nobody knows anything about their habits. I've heard rumors they eat the slaves they sometimes take away. They usually never come back. Or maybe they don't eat at all." He banged the tabletop with his fist. "There are days when I feel like ripping one of them apart and eating him myself just to get some fresh meat."

"Be careful what you say," Stark warned. "They can read your mind and they probably have listening devices everywhere."

"You can bet on that. Nothing happening here stays unobserved. Everything is recorded and stored in the Central Electronic Brain underground."

"Everything?" Stark stared at the big man. "Are you saying *everything* we do and say is recorded and stored?"

Corbo's wide grin did not inspire Stark. "Day and night, my wild friend; they know about your nightly sexual encounters."

"Those filthy devils! That is immoral in my mind."

"I wouldn't worry about that," Akros said soothingly. "They don't care about your sexual activities. As long as you do your job during the day. Neither do they care about what we say and discuss. They know we're helpless and won't go anywhere. We are the slaves and they are our masters."

"Doesn't anybody ever try to escape?"

"Oh, sure. Usually the newcomers, but they don't get far. There is no place to run."

Stark put his chin into his hands and stared at the metal tabletop. "I can't figure this out. So many planets. Untold numbers of different life forms. Some of them probably highly advanced. All ruled by a few oversized brains. Is there nobody who can resist them?"

Borkuu, who had followed their conversation with interest, spoke up. "There exists a race of beings that has the ability to free us from the yoke of Kaloor and the others of his kind."

"Where is this race?" Stark asked, curious.

Borkuu sighed and spread his fingers. Stark registered unconsciously that he had six fingers on each hand.

"They are an old race. The people of that race command incredible powers. When a male and a female join in the holy union of their bodies, their minds meld into one mind and at that moment they are like gods."

"Then why isn't this godlike race doing anything about Kaloor?"

"Power demands responsibility. They are not using their powers for evil but instead they created a society without wars and conflicts. Greed and aggression were bred out of them a long time ago." Borkuu shrugged. "My people are developing along that same path."

"He's saying that the higher a race climbs up the ladder of enlightenment, the weaker it gets," Akros injected.

"In other word, they just lay back and let Kaloor enslave them and everyone?"

"You could say that," Borkuu admitted reluctantly. "They could do nothing else. Violence is not something they believe in."

"That is hard to swallow." Stark shook his head in disbelief. "Among billions of people there is not one that will resist being enslaved?"

"Actually, there are not billions. Not anymore. Only a few hundred thousand are left. Scattered across this star cluster. Kaloor destroyed their planet in an effort to eliminate the potential threat they represented."

"He destroyed their planet?" Stark shook his head again. "I can't believe nobody fought back. And you call that evolving? Civilized? Every culture has to be able to defend its existence. If evolving means that this ability is lost then it is better to stay a barbarian. At least that way you have no scruples killing your enemy." Stark stared at Borkuu.

The other man nodded slowly and seemed to study his six-fingered hand. "Maybe you are right. But killing another living being?" A shudder ran through his thin body. His eyes met Stark's. "That is something I could never justify."

"Not even in self-defense?"

"Not even then. Killing goes against every fiber of my existence." He looked around. "I don't believe we should be discussing this topic. The Melkos are surely recording everything."

Corbo, who had been listening without saying a word, let out a rumbling laugh. "I'm sure they don't care what we discuss." He rose. "I'm going to play a game of *Krii*. Are you coming, wild man?"

Stark nodded to Borkuu. "It was an interesting conversation. We'll talk again."

Akros also got up. "I'll join you," he said.

* * * *

Something woke him from his sleep. Opening his eyes, he listened to the snoring of one of his roommates and decided it was not his snoring that had disturbed his sleep. Then he heard it again and realized someone was approaching his cot in the dark. When he saw the softly glowing eyes, he sat up and whispered, "Feleena?"

The barely visible shadow reached his cot and touched his shoulder. Then she put a finger on his lips and joined him on the narrow cot. Covering his mouth with hot lips, she kissed him passionately.

He pulled her close and realized she was still wearing her coveralls. "Take them off," he whispered.

She wiggled out of the constricting garment. When she was naked, she pressed her warm body against his. He felt her soft breasts on his chest and stroked her naked back. "I've missed you," he said softly.

She kissed him again and ran her hands across his chest, down to his belly. He was already stiff, and she giggled when her fingers curled around his erection. "That didn't take long," she whispered and rolled on top of him, capturing his hard member between her thighs.

He groaned when her moist labia grabbed his penis and when she rubbed her slit over it. Warm liquid ran onto his thighs and she moaned. He closed her mouth with his and pushed his tongue between her teeth. She ground her hips against his and dug her fingers into his arms.

"I needed this badly," she whispered fiercely. Opening her thighs, she clamped them around his hips and adjusted her lower body to let him enter her incredibly soft sheath. Her orgasm had prepared her for his entry and he slid easily into her.

"Ahh…" she moaned. "You feel good inside me."

He put his hands on her round buttocks and held her, while she pumped her lower torso in his lap. It didn't take long until she had another orgasm. Whimpering, she quivered in his embrace and milked him fiercely.

He put her onto her back and fucked her with steady thrusts. His cot made creaking noises as he moved between her spread thighs, but he was beyond caring if anyone heard him. Fleetingly he wondered if the invisible recording devices of the Melkos could see and hear him, but even that didn't bother him. Not at this moment. Maybe later he would be concerned about it. Right now he was only interested in the pleasure he experienced in the woman's embrace.

"Don't wait too long," she whispered, her breath coming in harsh gasps.

"I'd like to enjoy you as long as I possibly can," he whispered back.

"I'm happy to give you this pleasure." She let out a loud whimper and doused him again with her discharge. When she calmed down, she kissed him gently. "I'm drying up. Come now."

He held her tight and let it build up. His climax approached gently, grew until it reached the point of no return. As his spermatic fluid gushed out of his throbbing penis, he crushed her to him until the pleasure subsided.

She lay without talking in his arms and stroked his chest.

"I'm glad to have you back, Feleena," he said.

She laughed. "I'm not Feleena. My name is Serina."

"Why did you let me believe you are Feleena?" he asked, a little angry.

"I thought it might add to the titillation." She chuckled softly. "And I assumed correctly. It did make you more passionate, more loving. Do you love that Feleena?"

He didn't answer immediately. "Maybe I do. I don't know. We have a bond, let's leave it at that."

She kissed him on the nose. "What would you say if I told you I knew where she is?"

"I'd say you're lying."

"No, I'm not lying. I do know."

"Where is she then?"

"Not in this building, but I can tell you which one."

"Are you certain?"

"She arrived today with the new arrivals. When I saw her I remembered our conversation and asked her name. I will tell you where she is tomorrow. Come to my room and I will take you to her." She chuckled softly. "After we finish our physical joining is the price you will have to pay."

"All right."

Chapter Eleven

The next day Stark's group was sent to another location. This time he didn't have to work as a guard, which was a welcome change.

"I want to check out something a bit further down," Corbo said. "Keep me company, wild man."

Stark was getting used to Corbo calling him "wild man". For some reason the giant had taken a liking to Stark.

They swam along the rocky wall, searching for the sparkle indicating Krestoll was near. Stark was a bit ahead of Corbo, when he suddenly saw a slim figure swimming toward the wall.

He stared, hardly believing his eyes; a girl.

Her hair flowed like a beautiful, golden veil around her naked body. In the light of his helmet her skin gleamed with a soft, golden color. As he watched her, Corbo appeared beside him. "She's not wearing a suit and no helmet, either," Corbo said.

"I've noticed that," Stark said, wondering about something. "She must be a native of this planet. I've met someone like her before."

"You have? Where and when?"

"When I was a captive of the Frogs. She was their queen. They called her *The Golden Goddess,* but her name was T'Phira."

The girl must have seen them, because she swam away from them with swift movements, toward the mountain that loomed before them. They swam after her, but she was fast and suddenly she was gone.

"Where did she go?" Corbo wondered. "She can't just disappear into nowhere."

"There must be an opening into the mountain," Stark said. "I wouldn't mind finding out where she went." He moved his head to shine his light at the rocky wall. There were narrow fissures and holes, but none of them large enough to hide a body, even one as slim as that of the girl.

Corbo grunted and called, "I believe I found an entrance. Come, and look at this."

Stark swam up to the big man. Then he saw it also. The crack in the wall was large enough for even Corbo to squeeze through, but not so large to be easily seen from a distance.

"Careful," Stark warned. "We don't know what's in there."

"Well, the more reason to check it out," Corbo said. He disappeared into the opening. Stark followed him with mixed feelings.

The tunnel was narrow. Corbo had already swum further into it.

"It's getting wider here," he reported. "Come on, we might still find her."

Stark caught up with him. He pointed at the wall. "Look at that stuff," he said.

"I've noticed that already. Krestoll. And a lot of it. But we can check it out later. I am curious where this tunnel leads to."

The low ceiling and the walls reflected the light of their headlamps. Tiny specks of brilliance sparkled like diamonds on a huge sheet of satin and Stark knew they had discovered a Krestoll mine of great value.

They looked for other tunnels leading into the one they were in, but the walls were smooth and without any cracks. There was no sign of the girl.

"There is only one way she could have gone," Corbo said. He pointed into the darkness ahead. "This way."

"I know." Stark was reluctant to follow the big man. "I don't feel like getting lost inside this mountain."

"Don't worry. As long as we stay in this tunnel we'll be fine."

Stark wasn't actually worried about getting lost. He was more concerned with what might lie ahead. There was no guarantee the girl was in here. She might have entered another tunnel which they had overlooked. He didn't mention it to Corbo. They'd find out eventually if the girl had come this way. The tunnel had to end somewhere.

* * * *

Her nude body glistened moist and golden in the sunlight and her golden hair moved lightly in the breeze. She smiled and beckoned. Then she arched her beautiful body and moved toward him. He wanted to touch her golden breasts, but she laughed and evaded his touch. Turning, she floated away.

He ran after her, but he could barely move. She turned and spread her arms. "Come." Her voice rang like a bell and when she laughed it sounded like the tinkling of a chime. "Come. Come to me and love me."

He finally reached her and fell into her arms. She grabbed his throbbing penis and with her soft hand she guided him.

He entered her and then he screamed.

The golden woman underneath him had turned into an ugly scaled creature.

"Come with me," the creature croaked and jumped away.

Stark laughed hysterically and then he cried, because he couldn't follow the creature. His body did not obey his command.

"It will be all right," a soft voice said. A gentle hand brushed away his tears.

His lids opened and he stared into a pair of big black eyes that looked at him out of a beautiful golden face. "T'Phira?" His words came out in a croak. He tried to sit up but lay still when a painful shock ran through his system. "What happened?" he managed to whisper. Then he realized that it was not T'Phira looking down at him.

The girl only smiled and shook her head. "I don't understand you, strange being. You probably won't understand me either. You will be fine in a short time. Just relax." She rubbed his arms and his legs, and then his chest. Slowly, her hands ran over his stomach. She gave a little laugh when she noticed that he was watching her.

"You have a strong looking body, strange being. A little different from ours, but the difference lies only in the skin and other minor things." She gave him an impish smile and touched his scrotum. "I find you attractive, you know. You look like a strong, capable male, and we do have need for strong males. It has been a while since I had my turn with a male. It is so much fun."

She took his penis into both her hands and stroked him gently. Stark felt the effect immediately. Within moments, his penis was throbbing in her warm hands. The golden girl broke into tinkling laughter. She bent down and kissed the tip eagerly. Then she stepped over him and squatted above him. Slowly, she guided him into the golden thatch between her thighs.

She gasped as she impaled herself on his stiff mast and started bucking violently.

Stark could do nothing but watch her supple body gyrate above him as she fucked him with great enthusiasm. His body was immobile. The only thing that seemed alive was his penis.

The girl pumped her lower body in his lap, snapping it back and forth. She had her eyes closed and moaned every time she sank down to take him deep into her hot sheath. When he erupted inside her she clamped down hard and, whimpering loudly, she accepted every last drop of his discharge.

When he was done, she opened her eyes and smiled sweetly. Getting off, she knelt beside him and resumed rubbing his body. "You will be fine," she told him again. "Only now, recovery will take a little longer." She looked at him from under long eyelashes. "I hope you enjoyed our sex as much as I have. I also hope you are not angry."

Stark smiled. "Believe me, I did. Too bad I was immobile."

She shook her head again. Her lovely features took on a questioning expression. "I don't know what you are saying but you sound friendly."

Slowly, he could feel the life creeping back into his body and soon he was able to move. The girl helped him and steadied him as he stood on shaky legs, trying to keep from falling over.

"What happened to me? How did I get here?" he asked.

She shook her head and shrugged her shoulders.

"Why can I understand you, but you don't understand what I'm saying?" he asked. Then it came to him as he remembered the translator device behind his ear. He thought it best not to let her know that he knew what she was saying.

Looking around, he saw that he was in a small room. The walls were smooth and bare and the room void of any furnishings, except for the mat on the floor. The one he had been lying on.

There were no windows in the walls. Yet it was bright in the room. When he looked closer he noticed that the walls were glowing with a soft but bright light.

The girl stood by the door and indicated that he should follow her. His eyes traveled over her nude body. She noticed his interested look and thrust out her breasts. Then she smiled sweetly.

She looked very much like T'Phira, the golden goddess of the Frog people, except she was much younger and more slender. While T'Phira had been a mature, experienced woman with a sadistic streak, this girl had an innocent look about her that made her more attractive and desirable. She was still smiling, and when her gaze wandered down to a region below his belly, she giggled.

Looking down, he realized he was sporting a giant erection and quickly placed his hands over his crotch.

She laughed and shook her head. "You are a strange creature. Why are you trying to hide something I already felt inside my belly?" She approached him and took his hand. "Come and let's go to see the *Wise Man*. He is waiting."

"Give me a moment to relax. I can't let anyone see me like this. I wonder what happened to my clothes," Stark murmured. "I'm also wondering how I got here."

The last thing he remembered was following Corbo inside the underwater tunnel.

When they stepped through the doorway, he saw two guards standing on either side of the entrance. Stark noticed both were males. They stared back, but he didn't detect any hostility in their stance and behavior, only curiosity.

One of them shook his head slightly as he looked at the girl. "You should have waited, Satara, until after the *Wise Man* tested him. He won't be happy."

The girl made a face. "Pah. That old man. What does he know about..." She wiggled her hips enticingly.

The two guards laughed at her antics. "Yes, he is a little too old for that," the second one said. He scowled. "But you should show a bit more respect when you talk about him. He deserves that."

She pushed out her split tongue. "He's still an old man." Pulling Stark with him, she said, "Let's see what the *Wise Man* has to say about you."

As they walked down a long, wide corridor, they were met by a group of chattering, laughing young girls. They stopped when they saw Stark and the girl.

"We heard there was another one, and we came to try him out," one of the girls said, accompanied by the laughter of the other girls.

"We didn't want you to have all the fun," another one said. She flashed Stark a bright smile and touched him boldly. "He looks capable enough."

"He is quite capable," Satara said. She stepped between Stark and the girls who were crowding him. "Keep your hands off him for a while. I'm the one he was following on the outside, so I claim him first. I haven't been with a male for a long time."

One of the girls pushed the other girls aside and stood in front of Satara, her hands on her hips, her ample breasts pushed out. Stark couldn't help but notice that she was tall and superbly built. "You are not the only one who hasn't been with a male for a long time. I don't remember when I spread my legs for a strong male." She inflated her chest even more.

She pouted. "In fact, you just had one and I am filled with desire, especially now that I saw this one."

Satara looked at Stark and then at the tall girl. "All right," she said after a moment's hesitation. "You can have him once, but only once and only you. I must take him to the Wise Man."

The tall girl laughed. "He can wait. This can't." With that, she gave the other girls a signal and before Stark realized what was happening, he was stretched out on the floor in the middle of the corridor. Soft hands and lips were all over his body. When warm fingers curled around his half-erect penis, it grew hard in the girl's hand.

A pair of soft but strong golden thighs straddled him and he watched as his hard penis was swallowed up by a tight, moist sheath. Hot walls began throbbing with gentle rhythm and began milking him, gently at first but soon demanding all of his strength.

The tall golden girl churned on top of him with ferocious movements. Her ample breasts shook with every up and down stroke. Stark watched them with fascination, concentrating on the pleasure generating into his penis by her lively pussy.

The other girls were giggling and stroking his body with soft, gentle hands. One of them bent over him and put her lips over his, forcing her long tongue into his mouth. The girl in his lap kept grinding and twisting and when he came, she let out a wailing scream. Then she collapsed on top of him, resting her body on her soft breasts against his chest.

"Whah!" she exclaimed. "I never had a male like him before. His sperm shoots into you like the fiery tongue of s *Sprango*."

Her friends pulled her off Stark and another girl tried to straddle him, but Satara pushed her off. "Only one," I said. She pointed between Stark's legs and giggled. "He wouldn't be any good now anyway."

They all laughed and, reluctantly, the eager girl got off Stark. She helped him up and brushed her cheek with her lips. "Another time," she whispered. "I can wait."

The Earthman gave her a weak smile. "You will have to wait, little nymph." Then he followed Satara on shaky legs.

Another group of chattering girls passed them. Satara stood between them and Stark as they came closer.

"You want him for yourself?" one asked.

"No, but he has had enough," she said forcefully.

"Actually, so have we," laughed another girl. "We just came from the other one. All of us had him or perhaps I should say *he had all of us*." The group of girls broke into happy laughter.

"He is quite virile." She gave Satara an impish smile. "Maybe you want to give him a try?"

Satara smiled sweetly. "No, thank you. Perhaps later." She patted Stark. "He did fine."

They walked on and stepped through a doorway into a huge stateroom. Tremendous pillars supported a high ceiling. In the center of the room stood a large basin filled with water in which a number of laughing and giggling young girls splashed each other. A group of older women sat around the basin, watching over the playing girls.

On a throne-like chair sat an old man, watching everybody with little interest. He looked up when Stark and the girl entered the room. He smiled. "I see you have brought a stranger to interrupt my boredom."

The old women stopped chattering and watched them come closer.

"He is strong looking," one of them said. She got up and studied Stark. Then she touched his skin with one finger. "He has strange pale skin with some kind of fuzz on the surface." Poking Satara with an elbow, she cackled. "How does he feel inside you? Or perhaps you haven't tried him out yet?"

The girl just smiled.

"If I were any younger," cried one of the older women, "I would like to feel his white thing between my legs." She laughed shrilly. "Maybe I will try him anyway."

Stark looked at her flabby breasts and shuddered inwardly. Then he looked at the young girls splashing in the pool. He smiled at the old woman. "I'd rather put my white thing between those lovely young thighs than your skinny, wrinkled ones," he said boldly, knowing she couldn't understand him.

She cocked her head and cackled. "He even talks." She looked at the old man. "Let's find out what he has to say."

The old man called to the girls in the pool, "Corassa, Plenu, go and get the *thought-caps*. Hurry."

Two of the girls climbed out of the water. They disappeared through a doorway and came back moments later, carrying a large box between them. They sat it down in front of the old man and walked back to the pool.

Stark watched them go by, his eyes riveted on their nubile breasts. It was difficult for him to judge how old they were in human terms, but they appeared to be old enough to make them desirable to a healthy male. One of them glanced at him openly and wiggled her hips in a suggestive rhythm, giving him a shy but knowing smile. Her golden buttocks were full and round and moved gently as she walked by.

Any other time he would have reacted to her sight but now he was too tired to think about sex.

The old man spoke again and waved his hand toward the empty seat beside him. "Come, Stranger, sit down beside me."

Stark followed his invitation and sat down beside the old man, who touched his arm with a gentle gesture, smiling. Opening the box, he took out two helmets. One he put on his head and handed the other one to Stark, who did the same.

"Welcome to Sorom, Stranger."

Stark had expected it, but it still shocked him to hear the old man's voice inside his head. It was different from the way the translator behind his ear worked. The computer inside the translator changed the sound waves of the speaker. As they hit his eardrums they created the illusion that the words he heard were spoken in his own language.

However, this was completely different.

The old man had not moved his lips. There had been no sound and yet his words sounded loud and clear.

"Do not be afraid." The old man's smile was friendly and assuring.

"I am not afraid," Stark said.

"You do not have to speak with your mouth," the old man said. "Just speak with your mind."

"You must give me time to get used to this way of communication." Stark concentrated on the words he formed in his mind.

The old man nodded. "You are doing fine." He smiled again. "We don't see any strangers anymore. I remember when I was young, the Elders talked about strange people from other places. Places far away. We didn't understand what they meant and most of us were not interested. I was one of the few who listened to their stories, but I have forgotten most of them. It has been a long time. Do you come from one of those far places?"

"Yes," Stark answered. "I come from a place called *Earth*, a planet far away from here."

"A planet," repeated the old man. "Yes, I remember now. That's what they called them…planets, but I don't understand what planets are."

The Earthman looked around him and nodded. "I suppose you wouldn't, locked up in this place. I assume we are in some world beneath the ocean. How could you understand if you never see the stars in the sky?"

"Stars!" The old man seemed excited. "Yes, they talked about stars. Little shiny specks of light you can see on the outside." He heaved a sigh. "We never leave here, except for a few young warriors who go into the sea to hunt. There is no need for us to leave our world. We have everything we need."

"How did I get here?" Stark asked. "I remember swimming inside an underwater tunnel and the next thing I know I am lying on the floor unable to move." He stopped formulating his words when he thought of Satara and what they had done, wondering if all of his thoughts were open to the old man's probing.

The old man smiled and nodded. "Everything you think about I know also, but don't be concerned. I perceive the impression that what you experienced with those young females leaves you with a guilty feeling." He shook his head in wonder. "You are indeed a stranger to our ways. You are fortunate to be so young and vigorous." He sighed loudly. "I wish I were still young, but I am old. There are few pleasures left to enjoy."

He was silent for a while and Stark received impressions of a young man surrounded by many girls.

Laughter.

Love.

Happiness.

Then the pictures vanished and the old man's voice came again. "To answer your question is not easy. There is a *doorway* into the sea. We don't know how it works, we just know it does. We step through the doorway and appear inside the tunnel leading to the sea. But most of us don't have any interest going there, only a few brave young ones ever do. The hunters and the curious ones. Not many of those around."

"But how did I get in here?" Stark wondered. "And why was I paralyzed?"

"You came through the doorway at the end of the tunnel. Why were you paralyzed? The doorway does that to you. Every unknown creature coming from the outside is unconscious. Sometimes creatures from the sea come through and some of them could prove dangerous if they were conscious. Paralyzed, they are helpless and we can easily dispose of them."

They were interrupted by a couple of girls who had come out of the pool. They stood behind Stark, giggling and stroking his back. One of them boldly kissed his neck and nibbled on his ear.

The old man smiled. "You are indeed very lucky. Even the younger ones like you, but then I can't blame them. You are a fine looking specimen of a male, strong and, I hear, quite virile. Apparently, there was another stranger with you, a ferocious looking giant. He also seems to be quite popular with the females. I must talk to him later."

He became aware of Stark's embarrassment and chuckled. Then he waved the two girls away. They left reluctantly, pouting and giggling as they ran back to the pool

The old man touched Stark's arm.

"Tell me about the worlds outside."

Chapter Twelve

How much time passed he didn't know. There was no day and night in this little paradise. The light was always on and the temperature always the same. How it was controlled nobody knew or cared.

When Stark finished talking with the *Wise Man* and he removed the thought caps, he discovered that he could still communicate with the golden people, even without the thought caps.

When he asked the old man, he said, "The thought caps do that to you."

"How?"

The old had only shrugged. "We don't know."

"Where do they come from?"

"They've always been here," answered the old man. "When I was young the Elders knew these things, but now we have forgotten. But does knowing really matter? We are happy the way we are and we don't need much more. Too much knowledge is dangerous."

Stark was surprised how ignorant the golden people were. They were like children playing in a garden. He noticed the females outnumbered the males. He saw many old men, but none as old as the *Wise Man*.

He didn't have much time to think about these things. The females kept him quite busy. Satara never seemed to get enough of him, and when she didn't demand his services, there were plenty of willing and eager females around.

Stark didn't see much of Corbo, who was enjoying the attention of all the young and willing females who searched him out. When Stark saw him for the first time after waking up inside the city of the golden people, he was somewhat surprised to see the clean-shaven face of the giant. But he shouldn't have been, because his own face was devoid of any hair after Satara had painstakingly and gently removed his beard with a keen-edged blade.

She told him he looked too much like a wild beast, even though she had never seen one. She found him more attractive without all that hair hiding his skin.

After that she shaved him every day. He didn't mind. The beard had made his skin itchy and given him a feeling of grubbiness.

For a while Stark was happy in the world of the golden people until the day he discovered that Paradise can be turned into Hell.

* * * *

Satara and Stark walked down the narrow path among the high plants in the Garden. They stopped underneath a tall mushroom-like plant. The girl sat down and leaned against the thick stem. She smiled up at him and let her slim, golden legs fall open to give him a view of the golden floss between them.

The Earthman ignored her evident wish, deep in thought. "Don't you ever work?" he asked.

Satara looked at him, obviously not comprehending the question. "Work?" she asked. "What do you mean by *work*?"

"Well...don't you ever do anything but lie around, swim in the pool, play, and...have sex? Don't you have to prepare food or do other things like...like building something?"

She stared at him with her big eyes. Shaking her head in bewilderment, she said, "I don't quite understand what you mean. We have enough food. It grows everywhere in the gardens. All we need to do is pick it. Sometimes we go outside into the sea and hunt for sea creatures or collect *Plaartum*."

"Who takes care of the gardens?"

"Nobody. They take care of themselves." She looked at him from under long lashes and smiled. "We do many things, but mostly we love, like maybe now?" She reached up and touched his penis.

He moved her hand away. "Later, Satara. I want to talk first."

She pouted. "Talk, talk; you always want to talk. What do you want to know?"

"You said you love all the time, and I'm not talking about the present since I've been here. When we met, you told me you hadn't been with a male for a long time. I've noticed there are not many young males around."

She laughed. "You don't know much, do you? We don't always need a male to love. We love with the *Sprango*."

"Who are the *Sprango*?"

She got up. "I will show you." Calling out in a strange sounding voice, she looked down the path, as if waiting for something or someone.

They didn't have to wait long. A large, green shimmering creature suddenly appeared among the plants and came toward them on silent clawed feet. Two protruding eyes glowed red on the scaly face. Coming closer, the creature clucked and stood looking at Satara, ignoring Stark.

He stared at the long penis hanging between the creature's muscular legs.

"That's a *Sprango*," Satara explained and clucked softly.

The creature came closer and touched her breasts with long, scaly fingers. Stark could see the penis thicken below its belly.

"Are you telling me you are coupling with an animal?" Stark asked, horrified by the thought.

"Oh, he is not an animal. The Sprango live in the caves below the gardens. Some say they are our brothers from long ago. There are not many females among them." She lay down on the ground and spread her legs wide.

The green male knelt between her legs and began to lick her genital area with a long, yellow tongue. Satara giggled, when the tongue entered her pussy. "You see, this is much fun. He is very gentle." She gasped and moved her lower body. Then she grabbed the Sprango's shoulders and pulled him up.

Stark could see the stiff penis of the Sprango and watched with mixed feelings as he pushed his reptilian cock deep into Satara's obviously eager pussy. Slowly, the scaly male moved between her spread thighs, clucking away happily, as he brought Satara to an orgasm. She bucked and whimpered in his embrace.

Helplessly, Stark watched as the Sprango experienced his own climax between the girls clutching thighs. The lean buttocks quivered as he shot his load into her milking sheath.

Satara stroked the ugly male's scaly head and, gently, she pushed him off. With obvious reluctance, he pulled out of her and rose. Before he turned to walk away, he looked at Stark. "May the *Gods of Pleasure* smile favorably upon you and lend you power and stamina, man with white skin. This female is always ready and eager for coupling. So am I." He pulled his thick lips into the parody of a smile. "I am not an ignorant animal. Just different from you."

Stark watched him walking away, perplexed and dumbfounded.

Satara laughed. "I told you." She beckoned. "Come and love me now. I am still in need of much love. The Sprango only left me wanting more. I want you."

He looked down at her nude body, spread legs and the dark, golden slit clearly visible between them. Shaking his head, he said, "I don't feel like having sex. Not after watching you with that...that ugly creature."

"He is not ugly, only different. Was what I did wrong?"

He stared at her innocent face. "It didn't seem right to me, but I know I am wrong. Since I left my world I have seen and done so many things I would never have condoned before, but now...I realize there are other worlds with different morals, different customs, and laws. I can't judge you by my standards."

He knelt beside her and stroked her cheek. "You have to forgive me. I can't change overnight."

"I understand. It is all right. We will love later when you feel like it."

He lay down beside her and pulled her close, kissing her on the forehead. "You are a sweet and innocent girl," he said gently.

She laughed her silvery, tinkling laugh, put her warm, slender arms around his neck, and kissed him hungrily. He could feel his body reacting to her warm, soft body. Giggling, she pulled him on top of her and spread her legs wide.

He found her moist and ready as she eagerly received him. His hard penis slid easily into her greased sheath and within moments she bucked violently under him. He felt his own pleasure mounting and he was ready to explode, when a loud scream interrupted the silence in the Garden. The shouting of many voices made him stop and roll off Satara.

She was still moaning and writhing, oblivious of the voices, her belly working in the aftermath of her orgasm. Opening her eyes, she stared unseeing for a moment. She seemed to realize that Stark wasn't inside her anymore. "What is it?" she asked, pouting a little. "You didn't..." She stopped talking and her eyes widened when another scream reached her ears.

Clutching Stark's arm, she sobbed, "The *Wild Ones* are back."

The passion in her eyes had been replaced by sheer terror as she stared at him.

"I don't understand. Who are the *Wild Ones*?"

As she clung to him, the girl was shaking visibly. "They come from the outside. There is another entrance, but we don't know its location. They come and get females for breeding. They always take the youngest and most beautiful."

"Why don't you hide?" Stark asked. He rose and pulled her with him

"It is useless," the girl answered. "They find us anywhere." She cried out and pointed a finger. "There!"

Stark turned to look in the direction she pointed. A horde of males had appeared between the plants. At first, they seemed to look like the males Stark had seen among the golden people, but as the first one came closer, he noticed the difference. He was bigger and broader, and much more savage looking. His bald head was adorned with a high fin that started at the bridge of his flat nose and ended up in the nape of his neck.

"Take her!" he barked at his companions.

Stark moved in front of the girl.

The brute stared at him. "Kill him and bring her!" He made an impatient gesture and turned to run down the path. The majority of his men followed him. Only two stayed behind.

They advanced slowly toward Stark and the girl, brandishing broad, sword-like weapons.

"Stay behind me," the told her and fell into a fighting stance.

The two *Wild Ones* came closer, their weapons lifted, ready to strike. As the first one reached Stark, he brought the sword down in a vicious arc. Stark had been watching the man's face and when he saw the flicker in the black eyes, he jumped aside, avoiding the sharp blade by a fraction of a second. Had he not acted so swiftly, his head would have been cleaved in half. He moved forward, grabbed the wrist of the sword hand with both hands and twisted, bringing up his knee at the same time to ram it into his attacker's unprotected belly.

The brute yelled hoarsely, obviously surprised by Stark's resistance. He let go of the sword, but Stark caught is before it clattered to the floor and rammed it into the wild man's stomach.

Pulling the sword out, he turned to face the other wild man, only to see the remaining one had thrown a screaming Satara to the ground and was trying to force open her legs. So occupied was he with his task, that he had not even noticed his companions demise. He had managed to pry open Satara's legs and proceeded to push his stiff mast toward her exposed pussy.

Before he could enter her, Stark reached him and brought the flat side of the sword down on the man's head. He collapsed into Satara's arms.

Stark grabbed him and heaved him off the girl. Pulling her up, he held her close for a moment and stroked her naked back soothingly. She clung to him sobbing uncontrollably, her whole body shaking.

She finally stopped shaking and smiled bravely. "Thank you," she whispered. Then she pointed to the two still bodies on the ground. "Are they dead?"

"At least one of them is. I'm not sure about the other one." He grabbed her hand. "Come on. Let's get away from here before the rest of them come back."

As they ran down the wide corridor that led to the large living area, they could hear hoarse yells and screams and the clatter of weapons. But above all the booming voice of Corbo.

When they stepped through the large entrance, they saw the giant standing with his back to a wall, confronted by at least three dozen of the savages. He presented a terrible sight. His mighty torso was covered with blood and his long fangs gleamed white in his open mouth as he brought the two swords in his brawny hands down on the heads of his attackers.

Stark gripped his own weapon tighter and, with a mighty leap, he was behind the enemy warriors. Before they realized that a new defender had appeared among them, he killed two of them, but then he was fighting for his life.

A sword was not an unfamiliar weapon for Stark. He had taken up fencing years before, but it had always been only a sport. Never had he ever imagined that some day he might need his skills to save his life.

He soon realized his opponents didn't know anything about the fine art of fencing. For them sword fighting was just hacking and stabbing. Parrying their clumsy attacks was not a problem; there were just too many of them and it didn't take long before they had him backed up against a wall.

The strange sword balanced quite well in his hand and he was weaving an unbreakable pattern around him. His must have killed half a dozen but they kept pressing on, undaunted by his prowess. They glared at him with savage and angry faces, their lips drawn back to expose sharp, pointy teeth.

"Ho, Wild Man," called Corbo. "Are you enjoying yourself?"

Stark smiled grimly. "Not as much as you apparently are. I hate violence."

"So do I," laughed the giant, "but I get very angry when I am interrupted on top of a woman."

Stark didn't answer. A sudden sharp pain in his left arm told him that one of his attackers had managed to break through his defense. He felt the blood trickling down his arm. His sword arm was beginning to tire and he knew he couldn't last much longer.

"Feleena," he whispered sadly. "I will never see you again.

Her lovely oval face framed by soft black hair appeared in his mind's eye and he could see her blue cat's eyes looking at him.

He felt the sharp edge of a sword bite into his right side and pain shooting up his arm. The fingers that held the sword went numb.

"Good bye, my love," he whispered. But before the sword fell from his lame hand, a strange vibration went through his body. He felt strength flowing into his arm and every fiber of his body. The pain was gone and so was his fatigue.

He changed from a defender to an attacker.

With a terrible stroke, he took the heads off two of his enemies; the next stroke took off the fighting arm of a third, while at the same time he pushed the stiffened fingers of his left hand into the chest of one of them, killing him instantly.

Within moments, he cleared the space around him. Jumping high into the air and over his opponents, he landed among them. As he came down, he swung his sword in an arc, beheading one, laying open the chest of another one and spilling the guts of a third one. As he landed on his feet, he turned in a circle, cutting four of them in half with his sword.

He had killed ten men in a matter of seconds without uttering a sound.

His enemies backed away from him, as he stood there, his naked body covered with their blood, the red-dripping sword in his hand, his eyes ablaze with a strange, terrible fire that burned like hellfire through every last fiber of his body.

Slowly he advanced toward them. There were only a few of them left. They stood facing him, their swords ready, but their savage faces showed fear, something they had never known before.

"What are you waiting for, Earthman?" Corbo roared. He was lying in a pool of blood. "Kill them! Now!"

Stark turned his face toward the giant and smiled gently. "I will, my friend," he said softly. "I will."

He turned back slowly and lifted his sword. "I will," he said.

Then he attacked.

Before any of them realized he had moved, all eight lay dead; their blood and the blood of their fallen comrades forming a giant pool on the smooth floor.

When the last warrior had fallen, Stark stood there, his sword lifted high above his head, his unseeing eyes staring at the ceiling, a smile on his lips.

Then, suddenly, he relaxed and dropped the sword. The invisible presence who had taken over his body was gone. The memory of the battle faded like a bad dream.

He gazed around like a man coming out of a trance. Looking at all the dead bodies, he fell to his knees and was sick.

A soft hand touched him gently. He looked up.

Satara looked at him shyly, almost as if she were afraid of him.

"What are you?" she asked.

"I am a man," he said. "Only a man."

She shook her head, fear still in her large, beautiful eyes, but also great admiration. "No," she said. "You are more than just a mere man. You are a god. You must be."

He stroked her golden hair gently. "No, Satara. I am not a god. I admit there is something strange about me, something I cannot explain. But just the same, I am only a man." He laughed softly. "You should know best."

A weak but still booming voice interrupted them. "Is there nobody here who is willing to help me?"

Stark looked up to see Corbo staggering to his feet. He and Satara rushed to the giant's side to help him up.

"I thought you were dead," the Earthman said gravely. He gave the big man an once-over. "Are you badly wounded?"

"I have lost some blood," grunted the big man, "but I don't die easily." He spat and kicked one of the dead savages in ribs. Then he winced and grabbed his side. "It takes more than these little *Barrats* to kill me." He looked at Stark. "If you hadn't come to my aid, they probably would have managed."

He shook his head slowly and gave Stark a strange look. "There is something about you that is very frightening, David Stark. Before you killed all of these savages, something happened. I can't put it into words. I sensed a strange, terrible force that radiated from you. I saw your eyes. They blazed like two miniature suns, and you moved so fast, it was impossible to follow events."

He pulled on his long, bloodstained beard. "Very mysterious and frightening indeed," he murmured, almost to himself.

Then he collapsed.

A few of the other girls came slowly closer. They threw fearful looks at Stark and seemed to shy away from getting too close to him.

"Please, tell them not to be afraid. It makes me feel like some kind of freak. And tell them to take care of Corbo."

Satara nodded and spoke to the girls. Coming back to Stark, she said, "I will tend to your wounds and clean your body. You look awful."

A nagging thought entered his mind. "What about the ones who came into the garden?" he asked.

"They fled when they saw the carnage you caused," the girl said.

"That's good," he said.

Chapter Thirteen

Satara followed Stark slowly as he entered the dimly lit tunnel. She hesitated at the entrance.

"We are not allowed in the *Forbidden Zone*," she said, her voice almost a whisper. "There are evil demons in there."

Stark laughed. "Evil demons exist only in your imagination. No wonder you never discovered where the *Wild Ones* enter into your world. Come and don't be scared. I'll protect you." He patted the sword hanging from his hip.

She hurried toward him and reached for his hand. "I am sorry," she said, smiling.

"It is all right, little one." Stark squeezed her hand gently. "Superstitions are not to be taken lightly. But let's go."

They walked down the long, narrow tunnel. The sound of their bare feet echoed from the bare walls. They couldn't see very far. There was an eerie, yellow mist in the air and it seemed to be getting thicker.

Satara stopped and put her hand to her head.

"What is it?" Stark asked. No sooner had he spoken when he felt an odd sensation going through his head, as if a giant hand had clamped around it and was squeezing slowly.

"The demons," the girl choked and pointed.

Stark stared ahead. Strange shadows moved in the yellow fog so thick now they could barely see each other. A giant dark form changing shape was right in front of them. His eyes watered and his head was on fire. The impulse to turn and run away was strong in his mind, but he refused to give in.

He drew his sword and stabbed it into the giant shadow, but his sword met no resistance. The only thing he encountered was empty air.

The mist had changed from yellow to purple and the shadows were swirling all around him, pressing close to him, but they fell apart when he stabbed at them with his sword.

They kept changing into grotesque forms. Some looked like giant birds with huge, staring eyes; some of them were enormous spheres from which darting snakeheads hissed at him. The next moment they all looked like a million tiny creatures floating in the air all around them.

Stark hacked and stabbed blindly with his sword but never met any substance.

Suddenly the purple mist changed to red and all of the shadows looked like Satara.

"Go back," they whispered in Satara's voice, but at the same time they beckoned. Their breasts grew to enormous balloons. Then he was smothered

96

by red, giant breasts with little moving mouths as nipples. "Go back," they said, moving their lips in unison. "Go back!"

"None of this is real," Stark told himself. "All of this is just an illusion."

He moved back and bumped into Satara, who was sitting on the ground, whimpering softly, her eyes covered with her hands. He bent down and lifted her to her feet. "Come on," he said with a heavy voice, his head spinning. "Let's go ahead."

She clung to him, and he dragged her along. His feet were heavy weights attached to legs that felt like stiff logs. They refused to move, but he forced them to walk on.

Suddenly, the swirling forms disappeared, the log lifted and the pressure inside his head was gone.

They stood inside a large room. Dials and screens covered the walls. In the middle of the room, on a raised small platform, stood what looked like a molded chair behind a cube that could only be a desk.

Satara clutched his arm. "I'm scared," she whispered. "This must be the lair of the demons."

"Nonsense." Stark had regained his self-confidence, now that he was in familiar looking surroundings. "This is nothing but a giant computer room. I think I'm beginning to understand a few things." He looked around. "This is incredible."

Walking toward the platform in the middle of the room, he pulled the girl with him. He climbed up onto the platform and sat in the chair, studying the dials and buttons in the cube in front of him.

He leaned back in the chair to look at the ceiling. As he did so, he heard Satara cry out. When he looked down, he saw a shape take form in front of him. It molded itself into the shape of a man.

An old man. Even older looking than the *Wise Man*.

The elder stood there, smiling; his hands open in the universal gesture of peace.

"Welcome, whoever you are. Since you managed to pass through the *Guardians*, you are either very clever or you have great courage. I have programmed the electronic brain to keep any intruders out of the control room by means of those illusions. Nothing must happen to the Great Brain or they will all perish. But permit me to introduce myself. I am Draan, the last surviving scientist of my race.

"The other members of my people have forgotten about the sciences. The young people somehow seem to lack the interest; all they want to do is play and pursue the pleasures of the flesh. They are like children and they don't realize how dangerous the path they have taken. Someday the electronic brain will break down and they will not know how to tend or repair it.

"We had a great civilization once. We even traveled to the distant stars, but that was a long time ago. Now our race has fallen back into the primitive ages. Some live like innocent children while others, the *Wild Ones*, live like beasts, killing and raiding."

He paused for a moment, running a hand over his golden hair.

Stark used the pause to ask a question. "How long have you been here? Why are you staying?"

The old man didn't seem to hear him, because he carried on, ignoring Stark's question. "I don't know how long I will still live. I am very old. I have seen many things, but now I get lonesome. No one to talk to anymore except for the artificial intelligence of the electronic brain. I am wary of living and I might follow the other scientists into the *World of the Mind*. That is the reason I am preparing this message, hoping some day in the future someone of my own race or some star traveler will find my communication and learn a little bit about our glorious race.

"There is a vast storage of information and knowledge in the memory of the electronic brain. Do not be afraid to touch anything. You can do no damage. Automatic safeguards will prevent harm."

He lifted a hand and smiled.

Then he disappeared.

Satara stood unmoving beside Stark, her fingers pressing painfully into his arm. When the old man disappeared, she gasped, staring dumbfounded at the place he had been standing only moments before.

Stark was also taken by surprise, but then he realized the truth.

"Where did he go?" Satara asked. "And where did he come from?"

Very gently, Stark removed her digging fingers and rubbed his arm. "He didn't go anywhere because he was never here. It was just a hologram which I probably triggered to appear when I sat in the chair."

He leaned back in the chair and there it was again, the swirling mist and then the old man standing in front of them.

"Welcome, whoever you are. Since you managed to pass..."

Stark got up and walked toward the image of the old man. He seemed real enough, but as Stark came closer, the old man didn't move out of the way or acknowledged Stark's presence. He kept on talking, his eyes focused on he chair.

"...but permit me to introduce myself..."

Stark stretched out his arm toward the solid looking image, but his hand met no resistance. It disappeared inside the image, presenting a strange phenomenon. His arm seemed to be stuck inside the man's chest. There was no other sensation except the visual one. His hand just disappeared.

The old man never stopped talking.

Slowly Stark pulled his arm out of the projection, fascinated by the realistic appearance of the hologram. The old man looked solid, real.

What an advanced knowledge these people must have had.

He looked at Satara, who stood unmoving, her eyes large and scared. It hardly seemed possible that this innocent looking girl with her superstitious fears came from a civilization that had been able to build all this.

"Don't be afraid," he said. "He is not real. He doesn't even know we are here."

The old man finished his message and disappeared again. Satara came running into Stark's arms. "Let's leave this place, please, David. I know I should not be here. This is the Forbidden Zone. Who knows what other demons might appear."

He stroked her soothingly and kissed her gently. "Nothing has happened to us yet. There are no demons here. In fact, I don't believe we will find anything alive. Believe me, we are quite safe here." He pointed at a door. "I'd like to see what's behind the door."

As they came near the door slid open automatically. The room behind the entry was small and bare, except for a number of molded chairs in the center. A transparent half-globe hung over each chair. Stark sat down in one chair and put his head into the half-globe. He motioned for Satara to take a seat.

With a little shrug she sank into the seat beside him. She smiled bravely when he touched her hand. "Don't be afraid, girl. Nothing bad is going to happen."

The door had closed behind them, and they sat in semi-darkness for a while, waiting for something to happen. When nothing did, Stark became impatient and he began to study the chair he sat in. He discovered a small panel in one of the armrests with a series of buttons.

Remembering the old man telling him that nothing serious would happen if he accidentally pushed the wrong buttons, he pushed one.

* * * *

It was a nice quiet place. The music was always soft and never too loud. He loved coming here.

He sighed and leaned back in his chair. Touching the hand of the girl beside him, he studied her lovely features and smiled. She was young; her full, up-tilted breasts almost burst out of her low-cut dress. Her golden hair spilled over her soft, golden shoulders, almost reaching down to her hips.

"You are so beautiful, Satara," he said.

She didn't answer, just sat in her chair, looking around with her large eyes.

"Good evening, sir. Can I bring you something from the bar?"

He looked at the waitress and nodded. "Yes, bring me a Martini and Gin and Tonic for the lady."

"Very well, sir."

He watched her walking away. Then he turned his head to look out of the window. He felt the cool breeze on his face and took a deep breath, enjoying the beautiful, quiet Fall-night. He could see part of the clear sky with the carpet of twinkling stars against the blackness of space.

The full moon was just beginning its journey across the night sky, and in the distance sounded the honking of a flock of geese on their way south.

He turned back to the girl beside him. "Would you like to dance?" he asked, but she shook her head. "David, where are we? What is this place? It is so strange. It scares me. Please, let's go away from here."

"Why, Satara? This is my favorite hangout. I always come here. Why don't you like it?"

"I don't know, David. I'm just scared. I have never seen anything like this before. This must be the home of the demons, like I told you."

He laughed. "Don't be silly, girl. There are no demons here. Like I said, I come here all the time."

Her eyes became large and she shied away from his touch. Putting a hand to her mouth, she stammered, "You, David Stark, must then be a demon. I should have known when you killed all those *Wild Ones*. No mortal being could have done that."

Stark laughed again, but then he became serious and scowled. "What did you just say? The Wild Ones? Come to think of it, there is something strange here."

Then he remembered.

"This is amazing!" he exclaimed. "Almost unbelievable." His thoughts were interrupted by the waitress who came back to their table and put two glasses down.

"Here you are, sir."

"Thank you," he said.

She turned away but turned around again when he called her. "Yes, sir, anything else?"

Stark smiled. "Yes. You."

"Me?" she asked.

"Yes. I want you. Come here."

"But certainly, sir. How do you want me...ah...dressed?" She giggled and took off her top, exposing her breasts. "Like this, sir?" she asked, moving closer. She sat in his lap and kissed him. He could smell the fragrance of her creamy breasts and felt the heat of her voluptuous body. Her gentle hands crept down his chest toward his belly. When her fingers curled around his manhood, he moaned and put his hand on her breast.

He knew he could tell her to get undressed and she would comply without questioning him. He could fuck her if he wanted to and nobody in the restaurant would even pay attention, unless it was his wish.

Dreams were like that. Most of the time the dreamer has little control over the dream, but during the short period between waking and sleeping it was possible to influence some of the things happening.

Of course, he knew this was not exactly a dream. It was more, much more.

"Take off all your clothes," he told her.

She slid off his lap and removed her skirt. She didn't wear any underwear as he had known already. Her pubis was smooth and fat, exactly as he had imagined. Kneeling in front of him, she opened his pants and took out his growing penis. Looking up, she put her lips on the tip and teased with her tongue.

"Am I doing this to your satisfaction?" she asked coyly.

He nodded as a delicious shudder went through his body. She took his hard organ fully into her mouth and sucked.

The sound of someone crying brought him back to his senses. He pushed the waitress away from him and looked at Satara, who sat crumpled in her chair, sobbing loudly.

"I want to go home to my people," she whispered. "I don't belong here."

"Leave," he told the waitress. "I was only testing."

"That's all right, sir. Whatever you wish." She rose, picked up her skirt and top, and walked away, hips swinging lazily.

He turned to the girl beside him. "Satara, don't you see. This is not real. We are in a world that was somehow created by the computer. It looks real, even feels real but isn't. This is nothing but an illusion. It has to be. That girl would have never done what she did back on Earth, in the real world. The electronic brain must take the information from my memory and then work an illusion around it. It is like going to the movies, only more advanced. Total illusion. This is fantastic."

She stared at him, obviously not comprehending anything he said. "I just want to get away from here, from this…this place."

Something took shape in Stark's mind as he realized something.

"I don't know how to get us out of here," he said slowly. "It seems we are trapped inside the computer."

"Can I be of service to you," asked a voice behind them.

Startled, Stark jumped to his feet. He turned to the speaker. Even before he saw him, he knew who it was.

"Welcome." The old scientist smiled and held out a golden hand.

At first Stark hesitated, but then he gripped the outstretched hand, which felt solid and warm. "I don't quite understand," he said, puzzled. "I was certain all of this was just an illusion. Now I'm not so sure. I assumed you were dead, but you look alive to me. If you're not dead you must be incredibly old."

The old man chuckled. "In a sense I am dead. I died a long time ago and yet I live."

Stark shook his head. "Your explanation doesn't make sense to me. Tell me, is this an illusion or is this real? Am I back on Earth, my home planet?" He paused suddenly. "Is it possible I've died?"

"No, you are not dead." The old scientist smiled, obviously enjoying himself. "You are quite alive."

"That's comforting to know. You didn't really answer my question. Where am I? Is this reality?"

"It is and it is not. But isn't reality nothing but an illusion?" The old scientist looked at him with kind eyes. "Let me show you some of the wonders of my race when it was great and glorious."

Without warning or any sensation their surroundings changed. Instead of sitting at a table Stark found himself walking among a group of strangers.

"I hear you have been to one of the newly discovered systems," said a voice beside him.

"Yes, I've come back," he heard himself answer.

"I hope you had a pleasant trip," a woman's voice said softly.

He looked at her and smiled. "How can anything be pleasant without you by my side?" He touched her hand. "I am glad to be back after spending an eternity on a savage planet among savage beasts." He lifted the stump of his right arm. "Although I will be much happier after they have re-grown my arm."

Stark looked with horror at the empty sleeve of the uniform he wore.

"My arm," he wanted to scream but no sound came over his lips.

My arm! What happened to my arm?

He stopped. His head felt suddenly dizzy.

"Is something wrong?" the woman asked and looked at him with her large, golden eyes.

"It is nothing to worry about," said the man who walked on her other side. He touched her shoulders. Her eyes widened. She looked down at herself. "Where am I?" she whispered. Then she stared at Stark and the other man. "Who are you?"

The other man smiled. "Don't be afraid." He looked at Stark. "Are you all right?"

The Earthman found that his body responded to his commands. Again, he looked at the empty sleeve of his uniform. "What happened?" he stammered.

"Do not be alarmed. This is not your body. We have temporarily borrowed these bodies from their owners." He waved his arm in a grandiose gesture. "Welcome to the world of my ancestors, Earthman. When my people were traveling the stars, yours were still swinging from the trees."

He laughed when he saw Stark's expression. "Don't be offended, my son, but it is the truth."

"Are you telling me this is all real?" Stark exclaimed. "Have we traveled back in time…into the past? How is that possible?"

"Don't ask too many questions when you won't understand the answers. Yes, we are in the past…or future. It is really irrelevant. At this moment of our existence, we are at *Now*. Let me warn you. Even though you are only a guest in this timeframe, your physical existence can be ended here. So be careful. Don't ask me to explain, just except."

They had kept on walking and when Stark looked around he took note of their surroundings. The ground they walked on seemed to be made of some hard, glass-like substance. The buildings that rose on either sided of them were low structures made from the same glittering material. Each building had a different color. He saw shades of green, blue, yellow, and red. When he looked up he noticed the clear, green sky, but it seemed unexplainably low.

His companion saw him looking up and seemed to read his mind. "We are not on the surface of the planet," he said. "The city we are in is beneath the sea, encased by a screen of pure energy. What you see above you is not the sky but water."

Stark also noticed the many different people that walked through the streets. Most of them were humanoids, but some of them were so grotesque looking they seemed to have jumped right out of a madman's nightmare. He shuddered, as they walked toward one of these nightmarish looking creatures.

It stood about ten feet tall, walked on six skinny, hairy legs. Its bald head with the three eyestalks looked like a hairy wart on top of a giant egg. A mass of thick tentacles were curled around the creature's waist.

Stark expected them to uncurl and wrap around his body to pull him into a crushing embrace, and he couldn't help but release a sigh of relief when they were past the creature without being molested.

"That being we just past belongs to one of the most advanced civilizations in the Galaxy. It is also one the most peaceful species."

"The tall, ugly looking creature?" Stark remarked, unbelieving.

The man beside him smiled and shook his head. "By now you should know better than saying something demeaning, David Stark," he chided. "A being might look ugly to you, but how do you think you appear in their eyes?"

"I suppose you are right," Stark admitted. "I apologize."

"There is much to learn, my son. I'm taking a phrase from your own mind; *don't judge a book by its cover.* Everything is relative, like time and space, reality and illusion, Heaven and Hell."

They entered a brightly colored building. There were many rooms inside; some of them were furnished with tables and chairs. Stark's companion chose one of the tables and said, "Please, take a seat."

"This looks like a restaurant," Stark remarked.

The other man laughed. "You are assuming correctly. This is a place where we can order something to eat. Life on this planet and on many others is not much different from life on your planet Earth. People may look different on the outside, but inside we are all alike. One thing we all have in common is the desire to eat. You can't sustain a physical body without food. And this body is hungry."

As soon as they were seated, two platters with steaming food materialized in the middle of the table.

"How...?" Stark looked perplexed. "We didn't even order."

"You don't have to order. You take what you want. When you are finished, the platter will be sent back to Central Food Processing. Nothing is wasted."

"But how did it get here?"

The man chuckled merrily. Stark detected a bit of smugness when the other man explained. "Our civilization is far advanced in this time period. You call this process *teleportation*."

"I see." Stark took a small piece that looked like a slice of vegetable and put it into his mouth. Chewing and swallowing it carefully, he gave a satisfied nod. "Tastes quite good. Where does this food come from?"

"Most of it comes from the sea. The waters are abundant with life and the people harvest vegetation and water creatures. Some of the food is imported from other planets. Take as much as you want and need."

Stark began eating with gusto, finding everything delicious. He also discovered that he was ravenous.

Suddenly he remembered he was not in his own body and stopped eating. "This is really incredible," he said, touching his body. "I enjoy eating and I just realized this isn't even my own body."

The old scientist laughed and stroked his belly. "I enjoy it also and I'm supposed to be dead."

Satara only nibbled on her food. She hadn't said anything the whole time. She just sat in her chair, her eyes large and filled with wonder. But mostly she looked scared.

Stark touched her hand reassuringly. "Relax, girl, and eat something." Her hand felt warm and soft and Stark noticed the body she occupied was quite beautiful and he found her attractive. He looked at the old scientist, whose host body was not old at all, far from it. He was young and handsome.

"Are there more cities like this one under the water," he asked.

"Oh, yes, many of them. Almost seventy percent of the planet is covered with water and the two small continents are mostly barren desert or hostile jungle. Nobody lives there. There is nothing on the surface except for the spaceports which are built on huge floating platforms."

Stark regarded the other man with thoughtful eyes. "How can a species that lives under the ocean and never sees the stars develop space travel?"

Draan, the old scientist, smiled oddly. "A good question, my son, but easily answered. My people didn't always live under water. Many millennia ago they lived on the surface, on land. At that time, only about half of the planet's surface was covered with water. Strangely enough, at that time they didn't travel to the stars yet, even though they studied and mapped them. One day the scientists discovered that a traveling rogue star was on a near-collision course with our planet and they forecast the end of the world. The huge mass of the traveler would cause havoc on the planet's surface and large landmasses would be ripped into space or sink into the ocean.

"Then there appeared among my people a great leader, a young scientist, unknown until then. He revealed himself as a Mindgod and taught us how to build large screens out of pure energy. Under his leadership the people built huge cities at the bottom of the ocean, protected by an energy screen. When the catastrophe finally hit, the people survived, and since then they have been living under water, even adapting to it, learning how to survive *in* the water. Before the Mindgod left he gave us the secret of traveling to the stars."

"What is a Mindgod?" Stark asked, curious.

Draan gave him a strange look. "The Mindgods are beings with ultimate powers. Sometimes they enter the physical planes and walk among mortals. They only reveal themselves at times of catastrophes, when the survival of a species is threatened or the lives of many people are at stake." His eyes were thoughtful when he studied Stark. "I thought you knew." He shrugged. "But come, I want to show you the spaceport."

They left the restaurant and walked outside among the colorful buildings. The many strange and different people he saw fascinated Stark. Some were dressed in brightly colored costumes; others walked around in drab, colorless cloaks. Some of the people weren't dressed at all, revealing sometimes grotesque, sometimes strangely beautiful bodies.

They had reached a round towering building that rose up into the sky, or what looked like the sky, and disappeared into the green mist. As they entered the building, Stark had the sensation of stepping into some kind of elevator. He found out shortly that it was indeed an elevator.

A huge elevator from the bottom of the ocean to the surface.

The room they entered was large with seats almost like in a theatre. It didn't take long until all the seats were filled and the journey to the surface of the ocean began. Stark became aware of a gentle jerk and then he felt nothing.

"Are we moving?" he asked.

Draan nodded. "Oh yes, we are moving."

"How deep is the ocean at this location?"

"In your measurements it is about eight miles. To answer your unspoken question, it will take approximately thirty minutes to reach the surface."

"Thirty minutes. Hmm." Stark did a quick calculation. "That's about sixteen miles per hour. What about the effects of pressure on your body? In fact, I've been wondering how it is at all possible to live this deep under the surface of the ocean."

"It is not a problem. Compensation is achieved through regulators. I could explain it to you in detail, but you may not understand the principle." He smiled. "I'm not accusing you of being an ignorant savage, but I'm aware of the level of knowledge your species has reached."

"I understand. I'm not really interested in the principle. It was just something that popped into my head. I've never done any scuba diving, so I'm not familiar with the problems of pressure a diver faces." He chuckled.

"Like many things in life most of us know about it but don't really know what it is."

He settled into his seat, watching the many different people he saw doing the same thing. Strange, how everything seemed familiar but yet was different from life on Earth.

Stark realized they had arrived when everyone got up and began walking toward the exit.

"Come," Draan said, waiting for Stark and Satara to join him.

When they stepped into the open, he thought at first they were on solid land, until he realized the spaceport was nothing but a huge floating platform in the middle of the ocean. There were huge buildings surrounding the landing field. He was dazzled by the many differently designed spaceships lined up on the tarmac.

After the passengers who had been on the elevator with Stark and his companions spilled into the open, newcomers entered the elevator to take the trip to the bottom of the ocean. As Stark watched them, he saw something he remembered seeing before.

A tall, dark-skinned man walked toward them and Stark studied him sharply. The symbols on his chest looked vaguely familiar. In addition, the man looked very much like an Earthman.

Draan noticed Stark's inquisitive and astonished look. When the dark man passed, he nodded to Stark.

"If you are assuming the dark man was from Earth, you assume correctly," Draan said.

"But that is not possible," Stark protested. "We don't have space travel on Earth."

"No, not now, but you had thousands of years ago, at the time of the Ancient Mayans."

"That's why I recognized those symbols. I've seen them in books, but I still can't believe it." Stark stared at Draan. "How is it that you know so much about my planet Earth, a small insignificant planet at the edge of the Galaxy." He hesitated. "Are you one of those Mindgods you told me about?"

Draan shook his head. "No, I am not a Mindgod, but they sometimes choose beings to serve them. I am one of the Chosen Ones. I have lived many lives on different planets, in different bodies. I have lived on Earth, as strange as it may sound. So you see I know Earth."

Draan was silent for a while then he said, "It is time for us to return."

Everything around Stark disappeared and his mind floated in darkness. Slowly, his awareness came back and he found himself sitting in a chair under a transparent half-globe.

When he heard a soft moaning sound beside him, he turned to look at Satara and touched her hand. She stared at him with unseeing eyes. Then her eyes cleared and focused on him.

"Oh, David," she sobbed. "What a strange dream I had. All the time I thought it was real, but now I am glad it was only a dream. Let's leave this place. It frightens me."

"Yes, let's get out of here," he said. "I also had a strange dream and it frightens me too."

Chapter Fourteen

Stark and Corbo had no intentions to leave Sorom, the city of the golden people. It was better than slaving away every day under water and digging for Krestoll. Here they were free. Corbo was recovering from his wounds and he didn't mind the attention from all the girls and even from the older women.

They treated Stark with reverence and he tried his best to reassure them he was not some kind of god but only an ordinary man. He couldn't explain how he had managed to find the strength to overcome all those Wild Ones; fierce warriors, who had terrorized the golden people for as long as they could remember.

"We are not afraid anymore," Satara told him. "Since you are here to protect us they won't dare to come again. And if they should dare, well..." She smiled. "You will slay them all. They will speak your name with fear in their hearts, but you will be remembered as a great hero in the legends our children will tell."

He felt uncomfortable when she talked like that. He did not find solace in the fact that he had killed so many men, even if they had intended to kill him and anyone who tried to resist them.

He knew that a few had managed to escape and word of his deed would certainly spread among the Wild Ones. Hopefully, this would discourage the rest of them from trying to pay the golden people another visit. He didn't know if he could repeat his feat again if that should happen.

Even the young men treated him with respect and awe. If at first they had more or less ignored him, now they searched out his company and wanted to know about the world he came from. They were curious if all men in his world were like him. They wanted him to teach them to fight the way he had done.

He taught them how to wield a sword but let them practice only with sticks, after one of them nearly killed his sparring partner. In time and with a lot of practice they might even be able to use a sword in real combat. It wouldn't do them much good though against an enemy as ruthless as the Wild Ones unless they could also acquire the ability to take a life without remorse.

He also taught them unarmed combat, something they could only master if they kept practicing it every day. Maybe some of them would be proficient enough to defend their people against intruders. He planted the seed; the rest was up to them.

He sat on a bench made from reeds that grew in one of the gardens, watching a group of young men fencing with their sticks, pleased to see that they seemed to enjoy the new games he had taught them. There may be hope after all for them to grow out of their apathy toward life and find new interest in learning new things.

But then he wondered if it was such a good thing. They seemed happy in their city under the sea, even with the intrusion of the Wild Ones who disturbed their daily routine at irregular intervals. Happy in their ignorance of the world that existed above them and hidden away from the rest of the Galaxy, but free from the yoke of Kaloor and his minions, the Melkos. What would happen to them should they be discovered or draw attention to themselves by venturing too far away from their city, trying to satisfy their curiosity of might lie outside of their little world?

He turned his head when someone touched his shoulder and smiled at the girl standing behind him. "Sakkira," he said, "I didn't hear you coming."

She laughed softly. "I am like the breeze that plays with the petals in the Garden."

"You certainly are." He grinned. "But you can also be like the wild water that rushes from the rocks in the Cave of giant pillars."

Pulling her lips into a small pout, she complained, "That is why I am here. You have not held me in your embrace for ten sleep periods. My water is so calm it may take a long time to stir it up again."

"Are you asking me to stir up your water?" he asked, chuckling.

"I am. I promise you won't regret it. I am ready to boil over."

He laughed. "That is something I certainly cannot allow to happen." He rose from his bench. "I can use some diversion right now. If you are so hot let me cool you down."

"I don't want to cool down," she said, throwing him a laughing glance. "I want you to churn my water with your flaming rod and create a fiery inferno inside my belly."

They decided to go into one of the gardens and lie down under a giant mushroom. The ground was soft and they were surrounded by tall plants with large leafs, hidden away from other visitors to the garden. Even though the golden people were quite open when it came to sex, Stark preferred privacy in his intimate encounters.

Sakkira pulled him into her embrace as soon as they stepped into the small space inside the leafy shrubs. Kissing him feverishly, she pressed her naked body against him. "Ever since I felt your stinger inside me, I have longed for it, longed for the feeling it creates in my body when you shoot your fire into my womb," she panted. "I need to feel you inside me now."

She put her arms around his neck, lifted her legs up and wrapped them around his lower torso. He cupped her round buttocks and supported her light body in his hands. His penis had grown and nestled in the crease between her buttocks.

Laughing into his mouth, she wiggled her bottom and managed to impale herself on his hard mast. "That feels good," she moaned, as she took him deep into her. Clinging to him, she squeezed her vagina walls with slow rhythmic movements.

He pressed her against the trunk of the mushroom tree and fucked her gently, making her come a couple of times. When his legs became tired, he sank to his knees and put her onto her back. Her legs flew open and he moved in and out of her with deep, slow strokes. He knew from previous encounters with her that she needed some time to warm up in spite of her claim that she was on fire.

It didn't take long until she bucked underneath him, throwing her head from side to side and uttering little shrieks as he increased his tempo and the force of his thrusts.

"Yess…yess…that's it," she cried. "The flames inside me are burning hot. They can only be extinguished by the boiling water from your dying spout."

He closed her mouth with his lips. Sakkira was a passionate young woman and copulating with her was a most satisfying experience, but she tended to talk too much. The only way he could keep her quiet was to kiss her during much of their intercourse. Thus occupied, she forgot about voicing her pleasure vocally and increased the movements of her lower torso, which added to the pleasant sensation her hot vagina created in his body.

He pulled out of her and said, "Turn onto your stomach."

She turned and lay waiting for him to enter her again. He sat on her legs and put his hard penis on her buttocks. Moaning softly, she squeezed her buttocks and captured his penis between them. He rubbed it back and forth, touching her puckered anus with its tip.

"Don't tease me," she cried out, her hands digging into the soft soil. He put his hands around her hips and pulled her up a little to expose her vagina. Then he lay on top of her and guided his penis back into her warm sheath. This position didn't allow for deep penetration but he knew that she enjoyed it. He liked the feel of her soft buttocks in his groin as he moved slowly in and out of her clutching love-channel.

She whimpered loudly and scratched the soil with her fingers as she experienced a shattering orgasm. When she calmed down, he pulled her to her knees and knelt behind her. Feasting his eyes on her curvy body, he fucked her with steady strokes, his hands around her fleshy hips.

He felt the vibrations rising up as his own climax approached and embraced the wave of pleasure rolling over him. With a harsh and triumphant shout, he exploded inside the hot interior of the grasping walls of her vagina, holding her body pressed into his groin. She squeezed her buttocks tightly together as she accepted his gift with loud hissing sounds.

Cupping her delectable body, he rested on her back, his breath coming in great gasps, his fingers digging into her soft breasts. He was aware of her heaving chest and listened with satisfaction to her breathing as she struggled to fill her lungs with air.

Her knees gave out under her and she collapsed. He fell on top of her and lay on her soft body.

"You are getting heavy," she complained, tightening her buttocks. His limp penis had slipped into the crack between them. She giggled, when his cock moved to the warm prison. "Are you not satisfied yet?" she asked, holding onto his penis with her buttocks.

He supported his body on his elbows and let her turn around. She laughed and captured his penis between her strong thighs. "I need to lick your stinger clean before I let you stick it back into my body." She squirmed under him and licked his chest, his belly and finally her mouth clamped over his semi-erect penis.

He moaned when she sucked it into her hot mouth, curling her long tongue around it. The tip of his penis touched the back of her throat, but she didn't gag. She moaned softly, as she sucked on him. He lifted his buttocks up to give her move freedom to move her head.

When he knew he would experience another orgasm, she put her arms around his thighs to keep from pulling out and let him climax inside her mouth, swallowing every last drop. She released him when his penis stopped throbbing and slipped from under him.

He turned onto his back, breathing harshly, his eyes closed.

This girl sure knows how to give head.

He smiled, thinking of the girls and women he had fucked. Some didn't like to give blowjobs; the ones who did were seldom good at it.

He opened his eyes when he heard the rustling of leaves being parted. The girl who stepped into the small opening was not a stranger to him. Her name was Corassa. She was one of the girls the Wise Man had sent to get the thought-caps when he first came to Sorom. Until now, he had not had the opportunity to copulate with her.

"I finally found you," Corassa said. "I saw you two coming into the garden and I knew you'd be hiding somewhere." She giggled. Kneeling beside Stark, she bent and kissed him full on the lips. "Is there some juice left in your big fin or has Sakkira sucked it all out of you?" she said after breaking the kiss. Her lips pouted. "You have ignored me."

Stark was surprised by her action. He had not paid too much attention to her because she seemed a bit young. He looked into her black, shiny eyes and smiled. "I have not ignored you, Corassa. I saw the looks you threw me and believe me I have admired your lovely body."

"Then why have you never come to me. I am ready for your big fin."

"You may be ready but are you old enough?" His gaze wandered to Sakkira. "Is she?"

Sakkira laughed. Then she nodded. "She is no stranger to a male's fin, as some of the girls like to call a male's stinger. She is ready to sample yours." She touched Stark's limp penis and chuckled. "It seems you are not ready to sample her nest."

She pulled Corassa into her embrace. "Give him time, he regains his strength quite fast. Until then you and I can play." Corassa lay back with legs spread wide. Sakkira placed her head between them and Corassa laughed delightedly when Sakkira thrust her tongue into her slit.

Stark was close enough to see Sakkira's long tongue darting in and out of Corassa's vagina. Both girls changed position after a while to make it possible for both girls to lick each other.

Watching them rubbing their bodies together and listening to their happy squeals it didn't take long until he was sprouting a huge erection. Looking at Corassa's pert buttocks sticking up as she knelt above Sakkira, he could see her fat labia and Sakkira's long tongue lodged deeply inside her vagina.

He rose and moved into position behind her. Putting his penis into the crease of her buttocks, he rubbed it back and forth. Then he moved it down and stabbed frantically. He felt the tip of his penis slide partially into the girl's wet sheath, felt Sakkira's long tongue moving like a snake along his shaft.

Corrasa squealed with delight as he pushed slowly into her hot channel. Sakkira left her tongue inside, wrapping it partially around his penis as he moved it in and out of Corassa's dripping sheath.

Feeling Sakkira's tongue caressing his penis inside the throbbing walls of Corassa's vagina proved nearly too much for him and his desire to climax threatened to put an end to the elation he felt. Fighting desperately, he managed to gain control and closed his eyes while he fucked one girl and received a tonguing from another girl at the same time.

Once he conquered the urge to come, he knew he would last for a long time and he enjoyed every moment of this wonderful experience.

He tired from the position and pulled out, reluctantly. Turning onto his back, he let Corassa straddle him. She grabbed his strutting penis and rubbed her clitoris over it, her eyes closed and her mouth open. Gasping, she took him into her and sank into his lap. He watched her nubile breasts as she squirmed on top of him, emitting little mewling sounds interrupted by soft hisses as she experienced little continuous climaxes.

He enjoyed seeing her supple body undulate above him, enjoyed seeing her chest rise as she gasped for air, and the pleasure her tight vagina created in his body. He realized that he had not seen one fat person among the golden people. All of them were slim and trim; the females beautiful, even the old ones. Their breasts might be sagging if they had been large in their youth, but none of them had flabby bellies. The males were muscular and lean.

Corassa opened her eyes and looked into his, her mouth open, gasping for breath. Her breasts became taut, small bumps as she tightened every muscle on her body. A shudder ran through her and her vaginal walls quivered around his hard penis. With a loud whimper, she doused him with her warm discharge, her gaze locked with his until her orgasm subsided.

Sighing, she let her body sag and sat for a long moment with her eyes closed. When she opened them again, she smiled. "That was amazing. I heard some of the other girls talk but I never imagined it could be like this. We must do this again."

She lifted up and stretched out beside him.

"I think he is not done yet," Sakkira said, laughing with delight. Straddling him, she took his stiff penis into her hand, guided it into her vagina, and rotated her hips in slow motion. Corassa giggled and put her lips over his. Her tongue sneaked into his mouth and probed its cavity.

Stark took great pleasure having one girl kissing him and the other giving him a slow, delicious fuck. Sakkira set him free and Corassa moved on top of him without breaking the kiss. He felt her moist labia mold around his penis. She moved her lower torso lazily in his lap and gently caressed his glans, letting only part of his cock into her hot sheath.

Feeling her tight pussy teasing him made him extremely horny. He grabbed her rotating buttocks and pushed his penis fully into her. She emitted a low moan as he penetrated her and snapped her hips back and forth with sudden ferocity, riding him like a wild beast.

When he was ready to erupt, he put his arms around her and turned her onto her back. Her thighs opened wide and she met his thrust with her own, taking him deep into her youthful pussy. His orgasm roared up like a tornado and carried both of them to incredible heights. She didn't hold back and sobbed in his arms as her tight sheath throbbed around his spurting penis. When she started to scream, he closed her mouth with his and grunted loudly as his spermatic fluid gushed into her.

He knew after this incredible climax he was done for a while. Suddenly quite tired from having sex with two passionate girls, he collapsed into Corassa's arms and tried to catch his breath. Her chest rose and fell with her own effort to breathe.

"Whah!" she finally exclaimed. "That was even better than the first time. Your seed is hot and powerful. Now I know for certain that I need to have you fill me again." She gave a little laugh. "But not today. You've exhausted me."

He chuckled. "I don't think I'll be able to walk. You two girls sucked me dry like a pair of vampires." He slipped off her and lying on his back beside her, he looked up at Sakkira who stood over him, a little smile on her pretty face. "Don't get any ideas, girl."

She laughed softly and sank to her knees beside him. Stroking his chest with gentle fingers, she said, "I am glad you are happy. It also makes me glad you don't reserve yourself only for Satara."

"So am I," Corassa said.

Chapter Fifteen

He sat beside the old man watching the children splashing in the pool. They were so carefree and happy, and yet Stark was strangely sad. They didn't even know how great a race they had been. This was all that was left…a few remnants of a once mighty empire scattered across the planet, some wild and savage and some innocent, living under the ocean without knowledge and with no real purpose to justify their existence.

He looked at the girl curled up at his feet and smiled. She was beautiful and he loved her.

The old man turned to him and patted his hand. "The gods have sent you to us, my son." He smiled. "But listen to what I'm saying. *You* are a god who came to us."

"Oh, nonsense, old man," Stark said. "I am as human as you are. I may look a little different on the outside, but I am still flesh and blood, like you. With faults and desires."

Satara stretched her supple body and smiled lazily. "You are a god but you are also a man. I should know."

"Not a mere man, my child," the old man scolded. "Only a god could have killed all those savages, therefore saving you and everyone else from a terrible fate. But it is well. We need the blood of a god in our race. Your sons will lead us to new great heights."

Stark laughed. "What sons? I have no sons."

"But you will." Satara smiled triumphantly, touching her belly. "I carry your son inside me."

Now it was the old man's turn to laugh. "There are at least three other girls who claim to carry the son of a god. Sakkira is one of them. Even young Corassa has announced that she carries life inside her belly."

"That's foolish talk," Stark protested. "How do they know they are not Corbos's children they are carrying in their bellies?"

Satara touched his leg and stroked it gently. "No, my David, They are yours. The giant's sperm is not fruitful in our wombs. Besides, I never bedded the giant, and neither has Corassa."

Stark was silent for a long time. He didn't know if he should be happy or not. If indeed the girls all carried his children, what would they be like? How would they be treated by their peers? They'd be strangers among these people, possibly even outcasts, unless they were fortunate to look like their mothers.

He thought of T'Phira living alone among the Frog people. Even thought she looked like her mother, she was not like her. The golden people might not have accepted her because her father was one of the Wild Ones. She had been cruel, not loving and gentle like her mother's people.

He turned to the old man. "Are there other cities under the water? Cities where people like you live?"

The old man shrugged. "I don't know. Possibly, there are but we have no contact with them."

"Where do the Wild Ones live? Do they live in a city like yours?"

"No, they live on the surface, but that is all we know of them."

Stark studied the children as they laughed and splashed each other. Some of them were a bit older, boys and girls near puberty. The older girls and women sat around the pool and played some kind of game. Some were busy weaving baskets out of thin reeds. He was surprised to see them work at anything productive, but then again, he shouldn't be surprised since he had watched the men make spears and other artifacts.

"Are you married?" he asked.

"Married?" The old man cocked his head.

"Yes. Are you living with a woman? Do you have children, a family?"

The old man laughed. "I have many children but they are grown up now. I am too old to produce more."

"What about your wife?"

"I don't understand the question."

"On my planet Earth, when a man and a woman fall in love, they decide to spend their lives together, start a family, become husband and wife. They perform a ceremony and promise to stay together, take care of each other if one gets sick, take care of the children they may have, be true to each other. A man will have sexual intercourse only with his wife, and the woman only with her husband. That's a marriage; a normal marriage. There are other forms of marriages but I won't get into those." He chuckled softly. "And not all couples stay true to each other."

The old man knitted his white brows together. "I understand what you are saying. Sometimes a man and a woman may choose to stay together for a while, but their bond doesn't stop them from having sex with another partner. To live together with the same person at all times must get boring."

Stark smiled. "There are many on Earth who share your believe. Those marriages usually end up in divorce, which is not always a good thing, especially if there are children involved. In an ideal marriage the children are taken care of by the parents, who love them and teach them about life. A child needs a loving mother and father to grow into a balanced man or woman."

"Our children are raised by their mothers until a certain age. After that they live with the other children."

"What about the father?"

"It is not always certain who the father is."

"Are you telling me the men have no responsibilities at all raising the children?" Stark had a hard time swallowing that.

"The men teach the young males. Things they should know. But men are not really needed to raise the children."

Stark shook his head. "On Earth there are many who believe single parents can do as good a job as married parents. Usually those are single mothers. Either they got pregnant by accident or sometimes by choice, but they don't want to get married for some reason. As far as I'm concerned they are wrong. Boys need a father figure, but that is only my opinion. It has been proven that children who grow up in broken homes usually have many problems later in life."

The old man sat silent, obviously thinking about what Stark had said. "I don't quite understand everything you are telling me. Maybe that thing about getting married is not so good after all if there are so many problems attached. Our children are loved by everyone and taught by everyone."

Stark sighed. "I've had to change my opinion about many things since I've been abducted from my planet. I realize what I've learned and grew up with is not necessarily right or wrong. Even on Earth there are so many different laws and customs. People have different beliefs. What is accepted in one country is frowned upon, even against the law, in many others. Right and wrong are relative concepts. On my planet people fight wars and kill each other over what they believe."

"That is a sad thing," the old man agreed. He squinted at Stark. "I cannot quite comprehend that because we all believe the same things. What kind of things would you dispute?"

Stark chuckled. "Maybe you should ask me what kind of things we agree on. The list would be much shorter." He looked up as Corassa came out of the garden, carrying a basket.

She waved to Stark and hurried toward him. Setting the basket on the ground, she smiled and said, "I've brought you some fruit. You must be hungry." She patted her stomach. "I've been eating more lately, since I'm eating for two. The little god inside me is quite ravenous." She threw a glance at Satara. "I brought enough for you. You need more food also." She giggled. Then she made herself comfortable beside Satara, who made room for her on the woven mat she sat on.

Stark took one of the oval fruit and bit into it. Chewing the sweet pulp, he gazed at the etched drawings in the far wall. He had studied them more than once. They depicted golden men and women riding exotic beasts. Some of the people glided on wings through a sky filled with animal faces and mysterious beings framed by circles of light.

"Do you believe in a supreme being?" he asked.

"You mean a god?"

Stark nodded. "Do you?"

"We believe there are many gods." The old man chuckled. "Why do you ask? You are a god."

"I won't comment on that. We've been through it many times. What I mean is this. Do you worship any gods?"

"I don't understand the question."

"Do you pray to one or more gods? Do you ask them for help or inspiration? Do you have a holy place where you gather and perform ceremonies and things like that?"

Shaking his head, the old man said, "No to all of your questions. What would be the reason? We cannot ask them for anything. The gods cannot be persuaded by us mere mortals. They watch over us and if the need arises and if they think us worthy, they will come and provide the help we need." He smiled. "You came."

"Not by choice, I assure you." Stark smiled grimly. "I am not a religious man but I follow certain principles. Basic principles that supersede all laws. I call them Universal Laws. On Earth, we have many religions. Most teach basically the same thing, but many believers have splintered into different groups and squabble over who is right. Through the centuries many wars have been fought over what people believe. Millions have been murdered in the name of religion. Men will go as far as committing suicide just to murder innocent people in the name of their god."

"Why?"

Stark shrugged. "I know the ulterior motive behind it all. Power. There are people who crave power above everything and they will do anything to achieve their goal. What I can't understand are the men and women who allow these power seekers to influence them to commit murder. Life is precious and holy and should not be extinguished lightly. Not for any cause or any god. A true god will never ask for that. That is why I did not celebrate after killing the Wild Ones. I know they meant you harm but that did not justify killing all of them."

"You had no choice," the old man said softly.

"I know. Sometimes we have no choice."

"This Earth you come from, it must be a terrible place," she old man mused. "The people living there are surely not civilized. They are savages and are not worthy the attention of any god. Only savages would kill each other for what they believe. Now I know why you left it."

Stark couldn't help but chuckle. "Earth is a beautiful planet, inhabited by many wonderful people. Not all believe in the wars that are fought. Most would rather live in peace with each other, but there are always those who force others to follow their ideology. I don't believe that Earth is the exception in the Universe. I've met one dictator, Kaloor. He's the one who had me abducted and he's the one who made me a slave."

The old man sat thinking. Then he said, "Maybe you will slay him the way you did the Wild Ones."

Stark didn't answer. He put his hand on Satara's head and stroked her golden hair. She looked up at him and smiled.

That night he didn't sleep well.

In his dream he saw Feleena beckoning. Deep down he knew she was his one and only true love. He ached for her embrace and affection.

Reaching for her, he felt himself falling into an endless pit. He wanted to scream but had no voice.

* * * *

He woke bathed in perspiration. Looking around he knew he was in a strange place, one he didn't recognize. The he felt soft arms around his neck and a pair of soft lips covering his.

"I knew you would come, David," cried the girl, hugging him again. Her blue cat's eyes were bright and shiny and filled with tears, but they were tears of joy.

He touched her wet cheek with his finger and stroked her black hair. "How did I get here?" He looked around again. "And where is this place? Maybe I'm still dreaming."

Feleena laughed happily and covered his face with wet kisses. "No, Darling, you are awake and you are with me. We are together again." Then she sobered a little. "We are in a spaceship bound for the next planet in the system."

"We are still prisoners of the Almighty Kaloor?"

She nodded. "I'm afraid so." Then she smiled again. "But now that you are here it won't be so bad."

He looked at the other girl who sat with her back against the wall of the small room.

She gave him a smile. "I told you I knew where you could find Feleena, didn't I?"

He chuckled grimly. "Yes, you did, Serina." He looked down at his body, realizing he was naked. "I hope they have a new suit for me. I lost my other one," he said, grinning.

"Where are you coming from?" Serina asked, studying him, curiosity clearly in her large cat's eyes. "You appeared out of nowhere. How did you do that?" She touched his biceps. "You've changed since he last time I saw you. You've become more…massive, more muscular. More savage looking. What kind of creature are you?"

He returned her gaze. "Questions I can't answer," he said. His gaze came to rest on Feleena. "Perhaps you can shed some light on this mystery."

"I'm not sure I can, David. I saw you in my dreams. I called out to you, like I've done so many times before. When I woke up I found you beside me."

He lay back and stared at the metal ceiling. "Another mystery for me to solve," he said with a low voice. Turning to look at Feleena's lovely profile, he said, "Ever since I came to you in the jungle on Earth strange things have happened to me. You are part of the mystery, Feleena. Are you certain you don't know why these things are happening?"

Her lips smiled but not her eyes. He saw something in them stopping his train of thought. Shrugging, he said, "Maybe this is all just one big dream I'm having and I'll wake up soon, back in my apartment on Earth."

"Perhaps," she said, stroking his cheek, "perhaps."

Chapter Sixteen

Not all planets are created equal. Some are worse than others are, and some are just dreadful. Stark didn't know yet how he should categorize his new home. He took a few shallow breaths to let his system adapt to the conditions as he followed the other slaves out of the spaceship.

The sky was tinged with red. A strong wind blew across the tarmac, bringing with it clouds of dust that clung to his newly acquired coveralls, painting them purple.

"I'm not sure if I will like it here," growled one of the other slaves behind him.

Stark turned to throw him a quick look. "Akros," he said. "I thought I recognized your voice."

Akros grinned, displaying long canines. Squinting against the glaring sun, he put a hairy paw on Stark's shoulder. "I don't remember seeing you when we boarded the ship, mysterious man from a planet called Earth. I was told you and your friend, the giant Corbo, disappeared while you were in the ocean mining Krestoll. We thought you were dead."

Stark shrugged. "You heard wrong. I'm here, aren't I?"

"Yes, you are. How did you get on the ship?" His yellow eyes were barely visible behind their thick folds.

"I teleported my body through space and flowed through the walls." Stark chuckled softly. "How else would I get in here?"

"How else indeed?" Akros didn't laugh. He regarded Stark with a solemn expression. "Do not tell anyone about this ability," he said, keeping his voice low. "But answer me this: Why would you teleport into a prison ship?"

"I was lonely for my friends," Stark said, still chuckling. "You don't really believe what I just told you?"

"Shouldn't I?" Akros asked. "Why would you lie to me?"

"I wouldn't." Stark pulled up the collar of his coveralls. He could feel the fine dust on his skin, making it itchy. It entered his nose, and he wasn't surprised when he heard some of the other prisoners sneeze.

Ahead of them loomed a huge squat building. It looked weathered. Small mountains of purple sand covered parts of the flat roof and he wondered when it would collapse under the weight of the sand.

There were other buildings surrounding the landing field. A number of vehicles stood in a cluster at the far end, near one of the buildings. They looked like large tanks with their huge wheels and tracks. It was obvious they were built for traveling across sand covered terrain. When he looked back, he saw the spaceship that had brought them standing in the middle of the landing field, looking lonely and forlorn in this desolate place, already obscured by clouds of purple dust.

The air was hot and dry, and nothing like the hot and humid air on the last planet, which had been unpleasant enough. The dust and small particles of sand in the air only helped to make it nastier. He coughed, feeling his throat already going raw from the dust he inhaled. He was grateful for the coveralls. At least they protected his skin from being pelted into raw meat.

He looked around if he could see Feleena and Serina anywhere, but couldn't find them. There were two more groups of slaves marching toward another building further down and he hoped that at least the girls would be in the same group.

When they entered the building everyone let out a sigh of relief. Stark inhaled the cool air with deep breaths, grateful for the change, but he knew this comfort would not last long. They hadn't come here for a vacation. He was a slave and things would only get worse from now on.

He scanned the group of slaves and estimated their numbers to be around forty. Most of them were humanoid in appearance, not much different from the group in the first ship after his abduction. The only familiar face was Akros.

"I'm hungry and thirsty," the hairy man complained.

Stark wasn't hungry but he could have done with something to drink. With regret, he remembered the jar of fruit juice that would have waited for him in the city of the golden people.

They're probably wondering what happened to me. Now they surly must think I'm some kind of god. He smiled thinking of Corbo. *I hope the giant protects them should the need arise.*

He watched a squad of Melkos carrying shock rifles marching through one of the doors. Their white faces showed no emotion or any signs of discomfort they might have suffered outside in the sand-laden gusty wind.

They stopped beside a small raised platform and stood at either side of it. Stark studied them with curiosity and noticed that, even though they looked straight ahead, their black eyes flickered from side to side and he knew that they were aware of every slave and everything that happened inside the room.

Devil's spawn.

He thought it and watched the Melkos for a reaction, but none of them showed any interest in him. Supposedly they could read his thoughts, but obviously they didn't care what he thought about them.

Damn cold-blooded sons-of-bitches!

A large man climbed onto the platform and stood wide-legged glowering at them from small, golden eyes. He wore loose yellow pants and a black coat. It stood open and displayed a muscular, hairy chest. His right hand held a heavy staff. He could have passed for human, had it not been for his red skin and the horns sprouting from his forehead. When Stark looked at the man's legs, he noticed they ended in large hoofs.

"Welcome to Sarras, Travelers." He spoke with a booming voice. "I hope you had a pleasant trip, and I hope your stay with us will be long and enjoyable." He laughed over his own joke. "You have all been fitted with translators. Is anyone here who cannot understand me; anyone who doesn't have a translator?"

After looking around the assembled slaves, he grinned and said, "I guess you all have one since no one put up a hand, paw, or claw." He burst out laughing and pounded his stick against the floor. The prisoners just stared; nobody spoke.

"What's with the solemn faces?" the big man asked. "I'm trying to lighten things up a bit. I was joking; some laughter would have been nice."

"Some joke," Akros growled beside Stark. "I haven't had a reason to laugh since those white-faced demons came to my home world. I am not going to laugh now."

"Let me introduce myself," the man on the platform boomed. "I am Torrow and I am the stationmaster of this spaceport. I answer directly to the Almighty Kaloor, which means he speaks through me. My word is law on this planet. Your life and welfare are in my hands."

"Tell me something new," someone in front of Stark said.

"You may have noticed that you have been divided into three groups. Your group will be transported to one of the new mines. Work will be hard at first and life will not be quite as pleasant as on some of the older mines. You'll be living in tents for a while, but as soon as you break through the shell of the mountain and into one of caverns, you will live inside the mountain, protected from the elements and other dangers."

He stopped and let his small eyes roam over the silent group of slaves. "The weather on Sarras is harsh. What you experienced outside is nothing but a breeze. It gets quite lively here sometimes. There are other dangers on this planet. You will have to be on guard against the *Rockeaters* and the giant *Dustserpents*. In addition to those dangers, the indigenous population is not exactly friendly. Some of the locals are vicious and warlike. They've been attacking our mining camps and murdering slaves, reducing our workforce. I have to be honest and frank with you. Our resources are limited. The Almighty Kaloor has sent us only a small number of his soldiers and few weapons. Once you are in your camp, you will be on your own."

His smile was cruel and mocking. "Don't believe for a moment you can escape. There is no place to run and hide for you. You'll be safest in the camp. This planet is hostile and you would never be able to survive on our own. There is no need for me to warn you. If you don't believe me, try to escape and I promise you will perish."

He stomped his staff. "You will spend the night in this building. Tomorrow you will be transported to your new workplace. In the meantime, you are free to walk around. If you are hungry, food and drink is available in the mess hall. You'll find it." He chuckled. "Enjoy your last day in comfort."

The slaves stood silent and seemed to wait for someone to tell them what to do next. Stark watched Torrow as he climbed down from the platform and walk away, flanked by the small squad of Melkos.

"I guess we're left to our own devices," Stark said to Akros.

The hairy man nodded. "I'm going to look for the food," he said. "I hope it's more than just cubes of fibers."

Stark laughed. "Keep on hoping, my friend." He walked beside Akros, thinking about the fresh fruit he had enjoyed only the day before.

Akros was not disappointed when they received their food. They weren't served cubes of fibers; instead, they were handed bowls filled with a chunky, brown substance.

Akros sniffed at the thickened mass and lifted his upper lip in a growl. "Now I wish this would be only cubes. I wouldn't feed this stuff to a three-legged *Leafripper*."

Stark dipped two fingers into the gruel and carefully tasted it. Shuddering, he stared at the bowl. He watched as the hairy man scooped out a large chunk and shoved it into his mouth. After swallowing it, Akros grunted. "It tastes better than it smells. You should try it." He scooped out the rest with his clawed fingers.

Stark shrugged. "I guess if I want to survive I'll eat what I'm offered," he said.

The water they drank from plastic cups had a strange taste and was warm, but it served to quench his thirst. He hoped he wouldn't get sick from it.

Most of the other slaves in his group were assembled now in the mess hall and eating. Stark had hoped that the girls would also show up, but to his disappointment he didn't see them. Their reunion had been short.

"The stationmaster said we could walk around," Stark said.

Akros shrugged. "Where would you go?"

"I would like to find a couple of friends who were on the ship with me."

"Who?"

"Two females."

Akros showed his large teeth in a grin. "Are you thinking of sinking your weapon into their sheaths?"

"I doubt I'll get the opportunity." Stark smiled. "I would feel better if they were in our group. Once we are away from here I may never see them again." He hesitated. "I'm quite fond of one of them. In a sense, she is the reason I am here in the first place."

"Are you saying it is her fault you are a slave?" Akros gave him a scrutinizing look.

Stark shrugged. "I wouldn't exactly say it is her fault, but I was in her company when I was abducted."

"It is her fault then. And you are still fond of her?" Akros shook his head. "You are a peculiar creature, my friend."

"It's a complicated story, one that I myself don't understand at the moment. Strange things have happened since I got here, things I can't explain, and there has to be a reason for all this. At least I think there is."

"You are a believer in destiny?" Akros asked.

"I believe everything happens for a reason. We all have been assigned some kind of task in this universe. Otherwise, what is the purpose of living?"

"We have a saying on my planet. *The gods have a mission. Mortals have only one purpose and that is to die.* You and I, we are only mortals, but sometimes we believe that we are like gods." He stabbed a clawed finger at Stark. "You, my strange friend, live in an illusionary world of your own. Maybe it is a good thing. It helps you to survive."

He grinned hugely. "Sometimes I have dreams of performing heroic deeds." He pointed in the direction of a small group of slaves sitting at one of the long tables. "See the buxom female over there. She is a fierce warrior from one of the more primitive planets. I am itching to stab her with my sword and bring out that fierceness as her strong legs crush my hips in her effort to squeeze the life out of my sword with her tight sheath."

Stark looked at the female and wasn't surprised Akros would find her appealing. Big and muscular, her hair wild and long, and her eyes blazing with green fire, she seemed to have jumped right out of one of the comic books he used to read when he was young. One of the *Monsters from Outer Space* types of comics. He shuddered thinking of lying in her embrace and finding his penis buried inside her sex-organ, wondering if she might rip it off its roots when she reached her orgasm.

"Yes, it would be a heroic deed to copulate with her," he said. "I wish you luck."

They left the mess hall and went back into the large room they had first entered. Casually, they strolled over to the door leading outside. Stark opened it and took a peek outside. After having his face bombarded by a blast of hot, sand-filled air, he closed the door again. "I don't believe I want to take a walk outside. The wind seems to have picked up considerably," he said. Then he sneezed and wiped the sleeve of his coveralls over his nose. "I hope they'll give us facemasks if we're supposed to work in those kinds of conditions."

The howling of the wind could be heard through the walls. Stark did not look forward to the next day.

In the evening, after another meal, all slaves lined up to receive their gear. After looking him over, the clerk picked a backpack from a pile and handed it to Stark. When he looked inside, he discovered it filled with items he surely needed, like a facemask, goggles, a skullcap, a pair of boots, another pair of coveralls, gloves, and a cape with a hood. He was surprised to find a collapsible knife and a large jar filled with some kind of cream. A large canteen filled with water was clipped to the outside of the pack.

He saw Akros rummaging through his pack. The ape-man took out the knife and studied it. Looking at Stark, he said, "Why would they give us a knife? I might just use it to cut the throat of one of those white demons. I wonder if they bleed like us."

"They do bleed." Stark remembered the one he killed in the ship. "But I don't think they have blood in their veins," he said jokingly, looking around for some kind of reaction indicating any of the Melkos might have overheard the hairy man's remark. He still wasn't quite convinced that they could actually read a person's mind. So far, he had not seen any evidence of it. He had only the word of Feleena and the rumors from other slaves.

Akros pulled the boots out of the backpack, took off the ones he wore and slipped into his new pair. It wasn't the first time Stark had seen his bare feet, but looking at the ape-man's huge clawed feet, he was again astounded by their size. It was probably a lucky thing that in this case the old adage wasn't true about the relation between the size of a man's feet and his penis. He had seen that one also. There was nothing special about Akros's penis.

"From all this stuff it seems that we are in for a pleasant adventure," he said.

"You got the facemask you wished for." Akros pulled the boots off his feet and put on his old pair. "At least the boots are a descend fit. I still don't know what to make of the knife."

Stark chuckled. "Maybe we'll have to go hunting for our food."

Not all slaves appeared to be happy with the things they received.

"What kind of blind, impotent *Stardevil* would put this into my pack? What should I do with this thing?" someone cursed behind Stark.

When he looked around, he saw one of the slaves holding up his skullcap. Stark could see why he was upset and questioned the wisdom of whoever put together his gear. You can't put a tight skullcap over a head covered with sharp spines.

"What are you complaining about?" another one wondered. "Does this look like it will fit me?" His eyestalks were turned toward the ceiling as he displayed his goggles.

"Maybe you should pull your eyes back into their sockets," the first one said.

"Ha! You know that I have no control over that. They emerge when I'm upset. Right now I'm upset."

Stark smiled and winked at Akros, who grinned back. "At least you and I are closer to the humanoid norm than those two," Akros said in a low rumble. "We don't have those problems."

Thinking of the hairy man's huge feet and claws, Stark questioned that. How could those feet be comfortable in the confinements of a pair of boots? He shrugged mentally. It was not his concern.

Akros was right in one aspect of his comment. He and Stark had much more in common than some of the others. When he looked at the rotund male with a short trunk for a nose, he wondered what kind of protection he would need to prevent him from breathing sand and dust. Or the tall, thin female with a long, flat head like a serpent, a sucker mouth, and three eyes; two on her forehead, the third one in the back of her head.

Boots and goggles weren't the only problem. One of the slaves looked like a giant ball supported by four short legs ending in a clump of tentacles. So did his two arms. Stark wondered fleetingly what sort of gloves he could wear, not to mention the boots. He wasn't certain what gender the odd-looking creature represented.

"You are right," he said with a touch of sarcasm. "We have no such problems. We are two lucky slaves."

They slept on the hard floor of the assembly room that night. Stark used his newly received cape to cover his body; and his backpack served as a cushion.

When he woke in the morning, his back was sore and he didn't feel rested, but he had a feeling this might have been the last comfortable night they had spent for a long time.

Following a quick breakfast of the same gruel they had eaten twice the day before, they were told to head for one of the vehicles he had seen after disembarking the spaceship. From close, they were even larger than they had appeared from a distance. Giant tracks covered the wheels and Stark had no doubt they were capable of crossing the sand-covered desert surrounding the spaceport with ease.

He saw the two other groups of prisoners leaving one of the other buildings and was hoping to get at least a glimpse of Feleena, if only to be assured she was okay. He spotted her in he first group that arrived shortly after his own group began to board one of the vehicles. She saw him almost at the same time and waved. He would have liked to talk to her, but he could only wave back and smile encouragingly.

Then it was his turn to climb into the transporter. He threw her one more look before he stepped through the entrance. Searching for Akros, he found him in a seat near the center. Akros waved and indicated the seat beside him.

"Did you manage to talk to your long-lost love?" the hairy man asked, smiling.

Stark nodded. "No, I only saw her. Perhaps we'll all end up in the same place."

Chapter Seventeen

To Stark's surprise, the transporter was air-conditioned. It traveled across the sand dunes with comparative ease. Stark suspected that it was supported by some kind of antigravity device, which kept the track-covered wheels from digging too deep into the sand.

When he looked around, he didn't see any Melkos. When he mentioned this to Akros, he hairy man chuckled. "That is in a sense quite disturbing. It means that they are confident we will not even try to escape. It also confirms what the stationmaster already told us. There is no place to run, no sanctuary anywhere. We are condemned to stay on this dust ball for a long time, perhaps even die."

"I will not accept defeat as easily as that," Stark said, feeling defiant.

Akros laughed. "Perhaps you can teleport your body away from here. Where would you go though? The Almighty Kaloor is everywhere. So are his minions. Face it, my peculiar friend; the gods have played a cruel joke on you. They may have given you a gift but it is useless. It will only end in your death. If not here then on some other forsaken planet. There is no escape. The only thing you can do is laugh in their faces and accept your fate. Fight to stay alive as long as you can. That is the only mission you have. That is your revenge."

"There are other options," Stark said, stubbornly. "Remember, my views differ from yours. I cannot accept what you tell me. I will escape. I don't know when and how, but you'll see, it will happen. And if I can I will take you with me, if only to prove to you that you are wrong, my pigheaded friend."

"I don't quite understand what you are applying with *pigheaded*. My translator doesn't translate the word, only an approximate meaning. I hope you didn't insult me."

"No insult, Akros." Stark smiled, using the ape-man's name on purpose. "From now on I will refrain from using such words. It is easy to forget we don't talk the same language. Translations can easily lead to misunderstandings. I am baffled by this technology. I can't even imagine how these translators work."

"I assume you don't have them on your planet?"

"We have translation devices but nothing as sophisticated as this. This is way beyond our technology."

"It seems your species is even further down on the level of enlightenment as ours," Akros mused.

"I haven't been to your planet. I can't compare it with mine. Surely there are some things where we are more advanced than some other planets, even yours."

Akros shrugged his massive shoulders. "It is possible but highly unlikely. You told me that you don't even have space travel yet. It seems that a species develops at the same rate in every aspect. That is just the way it is. All levels of a species' consciousness are connected, one leads to another. You will never develop space travel if you haven't conquered harnessing the *Macro-powers* or are utilizing the forces of Antigravity."

"Well, we have neither," Stark said. "But what if another species interferes? For example, if your people land on Earth and begin to teach us how to do these things; what then?"

"Then an unbalance will occur. If you are not ready to accept and understand the forces shaping your species then it will lead to certain disaster. To yield great powers a species needs to be mature enough to keep from using them in a destructive manner."

"And your species is mature enough to handle great powers?" Stark asked.

Akros emitted a low grunt and smiled. "I have questioned that many times," he said. "Believe me, mine isn't the only one I question."

"You are quite a philosopher." Stark threw his companion a quick sidelong glance, taking in the hairy face, flat nose, and protruding chin. "Never judge a book by its cover," he murmured under his breath.

"I don't understand the meaning of what you said." Akros showed his long canines and studied Stark with his yellow eyes. "Sometimes you talk in riddles."

"It is nothing. I was only talking to myself."

"That is something I never do. What is the point? Are you possibly two minds in one body?"

"Not that I'm aware of. We humans do that sometimes." He laughed. "Actually, we do that a lot. I do that a lot. Don't ask me why."

"You are a strange creature, David Stark. Too bad we are not on my home world. I would have liked to study you. You are an enigma."

Stark grinned. "I guess everything is relative. You have no idea how much of an enigma you are to me. On my world…"

He was interrupted in mid sentence by a shudder running through the vehicle. It lurched forward, then swayed, threatening to tip over, and came to a halt. Some of the slaves began shouting and jumped from their seats.

Stark looked out of the window when he heard a rapid hammering that sounded like gunfire. The vehicle had stopped between two large sand dunes. On top of one of the dunes stood a contraption that looked like a cross between a ship and a tanker. It had a number of square sails in the front. They were rolled up halfway on their short masts. *Sandship* was the first thing that popped into his mind.

He saw a number of figures dressed in long robes, hoods drawn over their heads, as they came scrambling down the sand dune toward the transporter. What they carried in their hands were unmistakably rifles.

One of them stopped, knelt and aimed his rifle at the transporter. It seemed to Stark that he was the target, and he ducked away from the window. Beside him, Akros did the same. A sharp metallic sound told him that the bullet had hit the side of their vehicle.

"There is no need to panic," a loud voice sounded from the front.

Stark searched for the speaker and saw a man in a black uniform standing on one of the seats. He carried a weapon in one hand. "As you may have noticed, we are under attack, but there is nothing to worry about. We have superior weapons and we will deal with the aggressors. Just sit tight and let us handle it. There is nothing you can do. Nothing you should do. The projectiles ejected by the primitive weapons of the natives will not penetrate the walls and windows of the transporter. You are completely safe."

"I hope so," Stark said under his breath. When he brought his attention back to the attackers outside, he glanced at the Sandship as it stood like a menacing alien metal monster on the mountain of purple sand. He didn't care much for what he thought he saw on deck of the ship. "Damn!" he cursed loudly. "That looks like a cannon."

A bright flame shooting out of the front of the *cannon* and a loud boom confirmed his suspicion. He saw a large black ball streaking toward him, and a split-second later the vehicle rocked again as the cannonball smashed into the side of the transporter. When he saw the large dent in the wall right above him, he did not feel safe at all.

The robed figures had reached the transporter and started climbing up on the side of the vehicle onto the roof. Stark caught a glimpse of a brutish face inside a hood. He thought he saw two glowing eyes staring at him momentarily through the glass before the marauder disappeared from view. The last thing he saw was a pair of long-toed, clawed feet, looking suspiciously like Akros' feet, only longer and slimmer. No shoes would fit those feet.

"Are those your relatives come to rescue you?" he said jokingly to Akros, who could not have missed the scrambling feet.

The ape-man displayed his teeth in a grimace. "My people are not warlike, not anymore. In addition, we've progressed past the use of primitive projectile weapons. If those were my people, they would slice this container open like a tube filled with *moon apples*."

Stark heard them pounding on the roof as they tried to get into the interior of the transporter. He remembered the knife in his backpack and thought it might be a good idea to get it, but a knife was not much defense against a man with a rifle. A throwing-knife might possibly give him a chance, but he had never been efficient with throwing knives at another man.

He smiled grimly. *Give me a gun and a target and I won't miss.* He had been a sharpshooter in the army, and he had done some hunting for deer and moose up in Canada a few years back, but living in a large city doesn't allow much opportunity to spend time in the woods. A man gets rusty.

He wasn't even sure anymore about his unarmed combat skills. He had not kept up his training after being discharged from the army.

"What about those superior weapons we are supposed to have? Why aren't they being deployed?" Stark looked for the man in the black uniform. He was still standing on the seat, staring out of the window. Two other men in black stood beside him. They also watched the action outside through the window.

"Why aren't we shooting back?" Stark yelled.

The man turned and stared. Stark noticed he was of the same species as the stationmaster. "We will as soon as the *Defender* arrives. Be patient. As I said before, there is nothing to worry about."

"Who the hell is the *Defender*?" Stark put the question to Akros.

The ape-man shrugged. "I can't answer that. I guess we'll just have to wait and see. Let's hope our insistent guests don't manage to open a hole in the ceiling before he arrives."

A loud boom and the subsequent rocking of the transporter as another cannonball hit caused a few other slaves to complain about the lack of response from the black-clad guards.

The Sandship moved forward, edging closer. One of its sails suddenly exploded and part of the mast splintered. A cheer rose up inside the transporter when a second mast folded over, spreading the sail over the deck of the Sandship.

"It seems the cavalry has arrived," Stark said. He looked out of the window, trying to get a glimpse of their rescuer. He didn't see anything at first, but then a saucer-like aircraft landed on top of one of the dunes. It advanced on long legs toward the enemy and fired another salve into the now retreating ship, hitting part of the trailer the ship was pulling. A gaping hole appeared in the trailer's side.

Stark noticed that the hammering above their heads had ceased. Then he saw the hooded marauders jumping into the sand and fleeing.

The aircraft, Stark assumed it was the promised Defender, didn't pay any attention to the attackers running through the sand toward their ship. They reached their ship and scampered on deck. Then the Sandship began to move away.

The Defender didn't fire another shot but just sat on top of a sand dune, like a huge spider, watching its victim.

"Why don't they destroy that ship?" Akros voiced Stark's unspoken question.

The guard must have heard Akros, because he looked in Stark's and Akros' direction and said, "We don't want to antagonize them needlessly."

"Why? Are you afraid of them?" Akros challenged him.

"We are not afraid of anyone. That's just the way it is." The guard glared at Akros then he climbed down from the seat. "Everyone relax. We'll move on."

As the transporter began rolling, the Defender folded its long legs, lifted into the air and swooped away.

Stark shook his head. "Strange way of dealing with bandits," he said. "They need to be taught a severe lesson, otherwise they'll be back. Next time with reinforcement. I wonder if they'd been as merciful had they been successful getting to us."

"Are you speaking from experience?" Akros asked.

Stark sat silent for a moment before answering. Forgotten memories rose to the surface of his consciousness. Things he didn't want to remember. "I used to be a soldier. I was a member of a special unit," he said slowly. "We dealt with terrorists and bandits. Sometimes we were forced to kill men who in their own eyes did nothing wrong. They did what they thought was their duty because they had no other way to survive, but it was our duty to stop them before they became so powerful that their existence threatened our way of life."

Akros nodded. "I abhor aggression. It violates my belief, but sometimes we cannot avoid doing harm to others. Violence is justified when your own life or that of your clan members is at stake, but, of course, we have no knowledge of conditions on this planet to judge the reason of what we just witnessed." He fell silent beside Stark who sat looking out of the window.

The transporter rumbled on across the rolling sea of sand. A strong wind whirled up dust and sand, peppering the windows and obscuring them with a purple film.

Stark leaned back in his seat and watched the alien landscape rolling by, like a scene out of a science fiction movie or part of a crazy dream.

Maybe I'll wake up and none of this has happened. I've had lucid dreams before where everything seemed real. Maybe this is one of them.

If it weren't for the color of sand I could imagine being in Africa in the Sahara Desert taking a holiday. Maybe a caravan of Bedouins will come into view at any moment.

But deep down he knew he was only daydreaming.

This was reality. Harsh reality. There would be no waking up this time.

He closed his eyes and thought about Feleena. They had been together only for a short time and yet, he felt a strange bond with her. When they made love in the motel, he had felt elated, alive like never before. It hadn't been just sex with a stranger he picked up on the side of the road. The connection they made so many years ago in the Brazilian jungle bonded them together. They had both been young and fallen in love as only young people can after knowing each other for such a short time. But their love had transcended time and he never forgot her.

Who can explain why people fall in love under the strangest circumstances and love each other so much, no matter what happens, nothing can keep them apart? He couldn't explain his feelings with rational reasons.

He had not lived a celibate life and saved himself for Feleena, but he had never developed the feelings he experienced with her for another woman.

His thoughts drifted to Satara, the golden girl, who carried his child. She told him he was the father, but he wasn't certain if she could be trusted. When he was with her, he thought he loved her. She was beautiful beyond description, kind and caring, passionate and loving; a child in a grown woman's body. *How can a man not love such a creature?* He felt pangs of regret for leaving her the way he did. *How could he protect her and her child, his child, from harm?*

...She turned over lazily and stretched her lithe body. Her full breasts flattened against her chest, making them appear smaller, as she reached with her hands above her head. Smiling wickedly, she put her foot into his groin and touched his half-erect penis, rubbing it gently with her toes.

"You are a virile male," she said. Moving down, she put her lips on the tip of his swelling penis and wound her long tongue around it.

He relaxed and waited in anticipation for her to suck him into her warm mouth, with her tongue still around his hard member. No human girl he ever had sex with could give head the way Satara could. Not even the most expensive hooker. Their tongues just weren't long enough.

He groaned as her hot mouth slipped over his straining penis. She unfurled her tongue and took him deep into her until the tip touched the back of her throat. She didn't gag, just worked her mouth and tongue gently around his throbbing hard piece of flesh. Holding his hips, she kept him inside her mouth until he couldn't hold back any longer. With a shout, he climaxed inside her sucking throat. She swallowed his sperm and sucked until his penis stopped ejecting its precious load.

Slowly releasing him, she licked him clean. Then she lay between his legs, her chin on his chest, her black eyes studying him.

"Do you love me, David?" she asked.

He put his hands on her arms and pulled her up. Looking into her eyes, he nodded. "How can I not love you Satara? You are so beautiful. Every male loves you."

She smiled. "You didn't really answer my question. That is not the only kind of love I'm asking from you. When I copulate with a male he loves me for what I give him, but he forgets about me after he leaves me. Do you forget about me when we are not together?"

He took her face between his hands and kissed her gently. "Never."

Her hand tweaked his penis. "What about when you put your mighty weapon into Corassa's tight sheath? Or when Sakkira drinks your sperm. Do you think of me then?"

"That is not a fair question, Satara. Obviously, I'm giving them my attention, but it doesn't mean I don't love you anymore."

She screwed up her face. "Sometimes I am confused. I love Sakkira and Corassa, but when I observe you with them, I have strange feelings inside me and that is something I never felt before." Her black eyes looked deep into his soul. "You told me about love, David; the special love between a male and a female. Is this love? Do I love you?"

He put his arms around her and held her tight. "You probably are..."

Someone poked him in the ribs and realized he must have dozed off. "What is it?" he asked.

"I hope you had a good sleep," Akros said. "We have arrived at our new home."

Stark saw most of the slaves getting out of their seats, carrying their packs with them. He pulled his own bundle from under the seat and quickly shouldered it, not exactly looking forward to getting off the transporter; at least they had been in air-conditioning For some reason he did not believe the new accommodations would be as comfortable.

Already the hot air from outside heated up the air inside the transporter. He moved with the crowd toward the exit. When he stepped through the door, he noticed the darkness outside and wondered how long he slept. Looking up, he saw the bright disk of a moon and the sprinkling of stars in the black sky.

His boots sank into sand as he jumped down. He pulled the hood over his head to shield against a sudden cool breeze; surprised and in a way happy there might be a relief from the day's heat.

When he looked around, he saw the desert ended abruptly against a wall of sheer rock. In the light of the moon, he didn't see the expected buildings. There was nothing but sand and the cliff.

Other slaves must have noticed the same thing, because he heard different voices asking about the whereabouts of shelter and sleeping quarters.

"Attention everyone!" Stark recognized the voice of the guard who had spoken before. "The supply transporter has been delayed and will be here by morning. Tonight you will sleep under the stars."

"Why can't we sleep inside the transporter?" someone asked.

"A transporter is not meant to sleep in. You'll be more comfortable outside. The sand is soft." He spoke with a sharp voice, not allowing any more questions or comments.

Stark looked toward the direction they came from when he heard the soft rumbling of another large vehicle approaching. Moments later, bright lights of a second transporter appeared over a sand dune and after coming to a halt the slaves inside jumped outside.

Hoping Feleena might be among this group, he started walking toward the other transporter.

"Where are you going?" one of the guards challenged him.

"I'm looking for a friend," he said.

"You have to stay with your group," the guard told him.

Stark gave him an annoyed look. "If you're worried I might try to escape, ask yourself where I would go. Do you think I'm stupid enough to run into the desert?"

The guard gave a low chuckle. "Are you?"

"Come on," Stark said, trying to sound friendly. "I just want to see if my friend is there. This might be the last time I have a chance to talk to her."

"A female?" The guard laughed. "All right, go ahead. But don't get any stupid ideas."

"Thanks." Stark walked away, seething inside. He would have liked nothing better than to smash his fist into the man's sneering face.

Chapter Eighteen

The slaves from the other transporter were congregating in small groups, discussing their fate. Stark peered into each group hoping to see Feleena or Serina among them. As he approached one of the groups, a hooded figure turned to look at him. They recognized each other almost at the same time.

"David!" The joy in Feleena's voice at seeing him made him almost run to her. She came into his arms. "Are you staying with us?" she asked, covering his face with kisses.

He shook his head. "I'm afraid they won't let me. I practically had to beg one of the guards to let me come over here. But this isn't so bad. You're not that far away."

"We're only staying until morning." She clung to him. "Stay with me tonight. I need to feel your arms around me."

"Is Serina with you?" he asked.

"Yes, she is over there." Feleena pointed. "We've become friends. I will ask her to join us. It won't be so obvious when we bed down together. Come, we will talk to her. She'll be happy to see you too."

Serina gave Stark a little smile. Putting her arms around his neck, she kissed him full on the mouth, gently, almost like a lover.

"David is going to stay with us until morning," Feleena told her. "Come and sleep with us."

Serina chuckled softly. "I'll join you only if you will share him with me."

"I will if he agrees." Feleena threw Stark a quick glance. "I share everything with one of my sisters."

"I have no problem with that," Stark said. "It is getting cool. Three bodies will be warmer than only one."

Serina rubbed against him. "Three naked bodies. We can make it real hot by creating some friction."

"Now you're getting the idea." Feleena laughed and gave Serina a hug. "Let's forget the situation we are in and make this a night of happiness and pleasure."

Stark saw others forming small groups and search for a place to bed down for the night. Most of them clustered near the protection of the transporter. There seemed to be little order and no organization, and he wondered about the lack of guards.

"Let's go over there," Feleena said, pulling Stark with her. *There* was a shallow depression beyond a slight rise and provided shelter from the cool breeze.

Feleena removed her cape and spread it on the sand. "We'll use yours and Serina's to cover up," she said. "If we snuggle close together we'll be warm."

Stripping off her cape and then her coveralls, Serina said, "We'll be even warmer if we're naked." She smiled. "Don't let me stand here all by myself. I'm already getting cold. Take off your clothes and join me."

Stark knew she was right, but he also knew she had an ulterior motive. To stay warm was not the only reason she stripped naked.

Feleena was undressed before him and used her coveralls to make the bed larger. Then she lay on top of them. Serina joined her but left room for Stark to lie between her and Feleena.

Shivering in the cold breeze, he took his place between the girls and pulled his and Serina's cape over their exposed bodies. He was quite comfortable feeling the warmth of a pair of soft breasts on each side of his chest and two hairy pussies caressing his hips.

"I hope you're not tired," Feleena said, trailing her hand over his belly.

Serina was bolder than that. She cupped his scrotum with one warm hand and squeezed gently. She giggled into his ear when his penis began to swell. Moving her hand up, she wrapped her fingers around his stiffening mast.

Feleena nibbled on his ear. "I'm happy you are here," she whispered. "I've missed you." She kissed him gently and rubbed her pussy against his hip.

His penis had grown hard inside Serina's moving hand.

"Someone is ready to enter a soft warm place," Serina said huskily.

Feleena laughed. "Since you did all the work I'll let you provide that warm place for him."

Serina slid on top of Stark and clamped her thighs around his hips. His penis jumped between the soft, wet folds of her labia. Laughing softly, she rotated her pelvis and teased the swollen tip of his penis taking only an inch or two into her slippery sheath.

He groaned and put his free hand on her buttocks to push her down, but she just laughed and pushed up her rear, releasing him. His penis throbbed fiercely with aroused desire. "Maybe Feleena wants it more than you," he growled.

Serina slid down his body and took his penis into her mouth, playing her tongue around it. Biting down gently, she grazed it with her teeth.

"Don't bite it off," he groaned. "I may still have use for it." Her tonguing made him even hornier, but he was determined not to come in her mouth. He wanted her and Feleena's pussy.

Serina released him and slithered up his body. Then, without any preliminaries, she lifted her lower torso and sheathed him with her wet, hot love-channel. He grunted and pushed up against her.

"I'm feeling much warmer now," she moaned.

His left arm was pinned under Feleena who licked his shoulder and neck with her tongue. "Take your time, Serina," she said, "but don't tire him out. Leave some for me."

Serina laughed and snapped her buttocks up and down, milking him with her hot, pulsating pussy. She gasped and buried her face in his chest. Opening her mouth, she bit down hard enough for him to feel pain. Her warm discharge ran down between his buttocks. He dug his fingers into her buttocks and held her against him. He couldn't control his urges and pumped his load into her, grunting with every throb.

Feleena kissed him on the mouth, swallowing his grunts.

He barely noticed when Serina slipped to his side to make room for Feleena. Without breaking the kiss, Feleena moved on top of him and, grabbing his stiff mast, she guided it into her dripping pussy.

"Ahh…" she moaned. "This feels good."

She moved above him with ferocious strokes. Having climaxed inside Serina, he knew he could last a long time, but he needed to be in control. Wrapping both his arms around Feleena, he pulled her against him and turned her onto her back. Her thighs widened and he thrust deep into her, fucking her with slow, deep strokes.

She whimpered and writhed underneath him, scratching his back with her fingernails.

The capes had slipped off a long time ago, but he was barely aware of the cool wind blowing across his naked, perspiring back.

"I can't just lie here and watch," Serina moaned beside them. She climbed on top of him and pressed her warm, soft breasts into his back. He felt the soft carpet of her pussy tickling his buttocks. She moved with him as he shoved his hard penis into Feleena.

"I'm getting a little tired," Feleena gasped under him. "Have your climax soon."

"How about now?" he grunted.

As the wave of pleasure rose up inside him, a feeling of joy and exhilaration came over him. His mind expanded and grew. He felt the tentative touch of other minds meld with his, lending him strength and powers beyond measure.

He was aware of Feleena's mouth against his throat and Serina's teeth in his neck. He knew they were sucking his blood from his veins.

He didn't care.

The universe was his for the taking. He was a god. What mattered the puny, mortal body sandwiched between two mortal females? What would it matter if they drained him of every drop of blood?

But deep down he knew they wouldn't drink so much to cause him harm. He didn't question what they did. It seemed natural and necessary. Blood gave life to mortal bodies. To a mortal body blood was what pure energy was to the existence of the universe.

Without blood there was no life.

He felt his blood pumping in his veins in harmony with the energy pulsing through the fabric of the universe. He went to the beginning of the cycle of time, witnessed the birth of the universe, saw it grow and expand into millions of galaxies with their millions and millions of suns, walked on uncountable planets, mingled with the inhabitants, experienced life and death...

He opened his eyes to find the stars had disappeared to make way for a dawning day. In his arms Feleena and Serina were still asleep. Shivering, he pulled the capes closer over their naked bodies.

He tried to sleep some more but his mind was too busy trying to digest what had transpired. He should feel tired after having sex with two passionate and demanding women but he didn't. He felt fresh and full of energy.

They had certainly given him a workout. Much of the night was hazy. Had they sucked his blood? He wasn't sure. When he touched his neck, expecting to find a sore spot, he didn't find anything. Everything seemed fine and yet...he couldn't shake the feeling that his memory did not deceive him.

He remembered dreaming; the feeling of unlimited power and great joy still lingered on, however the details of the dream eluded him.

Feleena moved in his arm and snuggled closer. Her naked body felt warm against his skin. He hugged her against him. It seemed each time they made love strengthened the bond between them. His mind turned to Serina who lay on his other side, her body as warm and soft as Feleena's. He liked her well enough, enjoyed having sex with her immensely, but that feeling of love he felt for Feleena was not there.

As if sensing his thoughts, Serina put her hand on his chest and stroked him gently.

"I had a wonderful time last night," she whispered.

He hadn't realized she was awake. Turning his head to look at her, he saw her studying him. "I don't want to come between you and Feleena," she said with a low voice. "She shared you with me out of love..." she hesitated, "for you and for me. Some day you will understand."

He smiled. "We've had sex before you knew about Feleena," he said.

"That was different. As you said, that was before I knew about the bond you two share."

"It is called *Love*," Feleena said from Stark's other side.

"Are you telling me you love me?" he asked.

She kissed him on the cheek. "That's what I'm saying. I know you love me. There is no use denying it." She laughed, making light of her remark, but he knew that her words were serious.

"I'm not denying it," he said, gently. "But there is more between us than just plain love. Much more and I don't quite understand it."

"What don't you understand?"

"We haven't known each other for long. It takes time for two people to really develop true and everlasting love." He paused, not quite knowing how to formulate what he wanted to say, because he wasn't even sure if it really happened, so he just came out with it. "Did you suck my blood last night when we made love?'

"What if we did?"

"It makes me realize that I know nothing about you. It also makes me wonder what kind of creatures you are."

Feleena laughed softly. "I've lived long enough on your planet to know what kind of creatures you think we must be."

"Are you what I think you are?"

She bent over him and looked into his eyes. "You mean are we vampires?" Behind her half open lips her teeth gleamed white.

He searched her face, for the first time consciously aware of the two thin fangs in her mouth. "Are you?"

She pulled her red lips into a smile, showing off her fangs. "Not the ones your stories tell about. We are not dead. Neither do we walk around at night looking for victims and sleep during the day inside a coffin. We drink blood not because we need it to live but to experience joy and pleasure. The only time females of my species drink blood is during the joining with a male." Her blue cat's eyes studied him. "Answer me this: Have you ever felt the urge to drink someone's blood?"

He took his time to answer, not certain if he should confide in her…and Serina, but he realized they would know if he lied. He remembered the fight with Corbo, remembered staring at his neck and the terrible compulsion to sink his teeth into the giant's pulsing vein. "Yes, I have."

"Have you given in to that urge?"

He realized by the tone in her voice and the expression on her face this was not just a rhetorical question.

T'Phira. You gave me more than just a good fuck that afternoon in your tiny island paradise. I can't explain what happened that day, but it was something I'll never forget. When I drank your blood my mind expanded and it let me reach a level of pleasure I've never experienced before.

"Have you, David?" Feleena asked again, her voice urgent.

"Yes, but only once."

Feleena glanced at Serina. "It has surely begun," she said. "I was not wrong."

"So it seems. I have noticed the change in him." Serina sounded enigmatic.

"You two are talking in riddles," Stark said. "I don't have the faintest idea what you are talking about."

"It will all be clear to you at the right time." Feleena sighed. "I only hope we'll be there when you need us."

Serina ran her hand over his chest. "I don't remember you being this hairy," she said.

"Maybe it's the air," he said, laughing. "Speaking of air, I'm going to get dressed. It is getting chilly. I guess it's the same on every planet. I remember when I was a kid and went camping. It usually got colder in the early morning, just before the sun came up."

"You are right. It seems colder than before." Feleena sat up, shivering.

He could see tiny goose bumps on her breasts. On impulse he bent his head and kissed one of her nipples. "If we were in a different place I know what I would do now," he murmured.

"Well, we're not in a different place." She sniggered. "Were it otherwise I might let you do what you would do." She pulled her coveralls from under her buttocks and wrinkled her nose. "They're all crumpled up and full of sand. I wish I had some nicer clothes to wear."

"So do I," Serina agreed. "I wish I were free and back on my home planet. I would go swimming in the lake near our farm and then I would spend the rest of the day riding my *rassa*."

Stark didn't know what she meant by *rassa*. Obviously it was some kind of riding animal, but the translator didn't give him a detailed description. "I would have no problem spending a day that way," he said, smiling. "Perhaps some day all three of us can do just that. Until then..." he shrugged, looking at the rolling sand dunes around them.

"What will we do until then?" Feleena asked.

"We survive," he said grimly. Rising, he put on his coveralls and hung the cape around his shoulders. He waited until the girls were dressed then he put his arms around both of them. "I'll have to go back and join my group. Don't give up hope. There is always a way out. Stay alive."

He slung his backpack over his shoulder, turned and walked toward the transporter that had brought him the night before, not feeling quite as confident as he had sounded.

While he worked his way across the mountains of purple sand, he saw the sun appear above the horizon, throwing bright light against the sheer cliff ahead of him. It was clear that the cliff was the beginning of a huge mountain ridge and the end of the desert. This would be his home for the next...weeks? Months? Possibly even years. Not a pleasant outlook for the future. Already could he feel the heat radiating from the sand as it absorbed the rays of the sun. The cliff would reflect the heat and make it even hotter.

He found Akros standing with a group of other slaves. The hairy man nodded to him when Stark gave him a nudge in the ribs. "I thought you might have teleported out of here," Akros said, grinning. "I wouldn't have blamed you."

Stark smiled. "How can I leave my best friend behind? Besides, what is wrong with this place? We have fresh air, free lodging and housing if the promised tents arrive. What more could a man ask for?"

"You seem to be in a good mood," Akros growled. Then he showed his teeth in a wide grin. "I saw you coming from the direction of the other group. You found your female companions. Did you finally get a chance to sheath your weapon?"

"I might have, but it's not something I brag about to others out of respect for the women involved," Stark said.

"Not even to a friend?"

Stark shook his head and chuckled. "Not even to a friend."

Akros laughed good-humoredly. "Your answer tells me more than you think. You're a favorite of the gods." His gaze wandered for a moment. "I don't have much hope I will ever be as fortunate."

When Stark looked in the direction Akros was staring, he saw the big, muscular female Akros had pointed out the day before sitting on top of her backpack, watching a group of men arguing over something, possibly her favors.

"You'll never know unless you try," Stark said.

Their conversation was interrupted by the arrival of another transporter. They watched it halt beside the other one, expecting more slaves to spill out. When the doors in the back opened, instead of slaves a number of vehicles rolled into the open. As soon as they were outside, they unfolded and changed into what looked like cranes and other construction machines.

One, a rectangular box, rolled onto the sand and opened up to reveal huge folded sheets.

"Get to work and start erecting the tents," a voice boomed over a set of speakers in the transporter.

"I guess he means us," Akros said. "It seems our free homes have arrived."

End of Book One